Commander ZERO

Commander ZERO

a novel by

David Neil Lee

*To Lynn
You must come out to
the Coast someday!
Meanwhile, there's "Zero"...
David Lee
July 19, 2012*

Copyright © 2012 David Neil Lee
All rights reserved

Tightrope Books
17 Greyton Crescent
Toronto, Ontario. M6E 2G1
www.tightropebooks.com

Editor: Heather Wood
Copy editor: Erin Sparkes-Brewer
Cover and typography: Dawn Kresan
Cover art: Keith Thirkell's *Starry Night Clayoquot*
Author photo credit: Maureen Cochrane

Printed and bound in Canada

We thank the Canada Council for the Arts and the Ontario Arts Council for their support of our publishing program.

  Canada Council   Conseil des Arts
for the Arts   du Canada

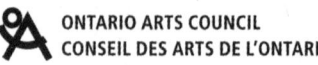 ONTARIO ARTS COUNCIL
CONSEIL DES ARTS DE L'ONTARIO

Library and Archives Canada Cataloguing in Publication

Lee, David, 1952–
    Commander Zero / David Lee.

ISBN 978-1-926639-47-5

    I. TITLE.

PS8623.E436C64 2012   C813'.6   C2012-901808-2

For Maureen

PENDER HARBOUR, pop 2,500, is a jumble of islands, bays and lagoons on the Sunshine Coast north of Sechelt. It contains the small communities of Garden Bay, Irvines Landing, Kleindale and Madeira Park.

PRAWN; *see* SHRIMP. **SHRIMP** is a marine crustacean with 10 jointed legs and a nearly cylindrical body. There are more than 85 species recorded in BC waters, occurring from the intertidal zone to depths exceeding 5,000 metres [17,000 FT.]. Different species prefer different habitats, from rocky bottom to mud and sand. Most species are bottom dwellers but some rise off the bottom at times. Seven shrimp species belonging to the family Pandalidae are important to commercial fisheries, [including] prawn (*Pandalus platyceros*).

The prawn is the largest of the harvested shrimp species in BC, growing to 20 centimetres [8 inches] total length. The minimum commercial size is slightly less than 14 centimetres [5.5 IN.]. Prawns live in rocky habitats and are typically caught using baited traps at 70–90 metres [200–300 ft.] depth.... [Japan is] the major market for more than 90% of the product landed in the trap fishery.
—*The Encyclopedia of British Columbia*

1. The drowned canyons

Between the mountains are canyons filled with salt water, and what I remember first is fishing in that water. The mountains are like the shoulders of women. The women are reaching under the water. They are searching for something there.

Under the surface, their stone arms are softened by the silt and sand that fills in the cracks and ledges of their steep rock faces. There are also the bodies, the living bodies and the dead, of the things that hunger and breed down there on the cold saltwater cliffs. The light from the sun does not reach far down into there; so that whether it is night or day, the bottom of the inlet is a different world than the one we have up here.

Even in daytime, that world down there remains a perfect place, it is so cold and so dark, and the creatures there drift along the mud or dart from rock to rock in a casual way, casting their feelers slowly through the dark water to see what food the current brings them. Except if it is time to strike or time to swim away from danger, to flee blindly down into the dark.

These drowned canyons are full of prawns. They like it best down there, where the dead things sink and drift and stay, and they will live there forever.

2. The prawns

Walter pilots the *Medusa Deep* past the rockfalls and cascades of foam bordering these dark inlets. When it is time for us to fish, he moves from the cabin to the helm controls on deck. He watches the depth sounder and threads a slow course this way and that, following the ledges of the underwater cliffs. He shows me how to help him, and together we string a line of baskets, made of black mesh and steel frames, clipped to a rope we unwinch far behind us along the rocky shore. The traps have to land on the ledges where the prawns will find them, or else they will just hang in the black water. That's no good, Walter tells me. Prawns are not swimmers, instead they skim along the bottom.

We set one string of traps, go to the next string and Walter uses the boat hook to snag the scotchman, the orange balloon that holds up the end of a string of traps. We pull in the string and, one by one, dump out the traps onto the sorting table, re-bait and stack them, ready to set again. Rustling and clicking their feelers and their bony legs, the prawns go into plastic cages in the live tank, which is a big deep freeze full of cold seawater. Then we lay the traps down again or take them with us, working our way up the inlets looking for the next good place, and then back down again. Walter keeps tabs on where the other prawn fishermen set their traps. By watching them come and go, he figures out how they are doing.

"Toby's set there Joey." Walter points up the inlet. I squint and stare, but all I see is the gray shoreline.

"He's got his traps strung all around that point," Walter says and he asks me, "Why's he setting so deep?"

Where is this prawn string anyway, I want to ask. I see dick all. I look and look and I feel the anger rising. Sometimes people bullshit me. They bullshit me because they think I will believe anything.

Then I see a tiny pinprick glowing against the faraway shore. It is Toby's scotchman—that colour is the same orangey-pink I see in the supermarket, that the store puts on its best deals, like day-old sugar doughnuts. You can see that colour miles away.

I take deep breaths the way they coached me at the clinic. I try to make myself stop feeling all pissed off, and no flames rise from the boat's deck. After a minute I can see that it works. I have kept control, and Walter has not even noticed, and I'm getting through this particular day.

"I don't know," I say. "I don't know why he's setting so deep."

"He's nuts to set there," Walter makes notes in his log book. "All his traps'll hang off in space."

Every day after that when we come back up the inlet, we look for Toby's scotchman off that point. He is catching nothing, Walter says. He can't be bringing up a goddam thing. Then, when Toby gives up and moves someplace else, we go and set in that spot.

3. Octopus tracks

Junk is a major part of our catches: hunks of rope, hose, net, fishline. Besides rocks and muck and prawns if we're lucky, we also get creatures that are not prawns. Sometimes a wolf eel, thrashing and clicking its needly teeth. Bony little stick men, tiny with no meat on them, we call "roach clips." Also "octopus tracks"—what we call empty prawn heads with only the helmet and the long, sharp nose spike left. The octopus sucks away everything else right down to the eyeballs. When he feels us starting to haul up the trap, he squeezes himself out through the hole in the top. We only know he has been there because of the empty prawn heads.

Sometimes the octopus is not so lucky. When we catch octopuses they look at us with their big cats' eyes. They are thinking, trying to figure out their situation. If they are little octopuses, we let them go. I toss them in the water—sometimes they cling to my sleeve with their suction cups and hang on, but eventually, as soon as their bodies slap the surface, they flip, suck in a big gasp of water and rocket back down into the dark. But if they're big enough to keep, we dump them in a plastic bucket full of seawater and weigh down the lid.

We weigh it down with a brick cinderblock. Otherwise... I've seen a big one pull himself out of the bucket and take off across the deck. If you watch on TV, they show octopuses that look like they're made out of rubber. But a real live octopus is like a big puddle of motor oil. It is a puddle with brains. When it wants to get away, it moves fast.

When I scooped this big one up, Walter took a picture with it clinging onto me like a giant cobweb. He was a good big one, so Walter stuck a paring knife under the back of his head and cut the brain stem.

"Is it dead?"

Walter nodded. The octopus went back into the bucket, and when we got to shore with our prawns, we sold him to a restaurant down the coast.

4. Bodies of water

In this country the shores are rock and the land never lays flat, and many a seafarer has thrown up their hands nosing some small vessel from bay to bay in fruitless search of sand or shallows where they might safely moor and come ashore. High or low tide, the ocean stays put, more or less. It is the land that seems to move, to entrap and confuse. The coastline faces to the west, and far past the strait, I see another coast much like this one with its shores and mountains. I am told it's a huge island. Only by sailing way up or down the strait will you get around The Island to finally reach the open sea.

Way out there, past The Island, the ocean only has one name, *Pacific*, but in here close to the land it has many names. Just offshore, the fishermen call it *the saltchuck*. That strip of ocean between here and The Island has its own name, the Strait of Georgia, and when it gets even closer to us, the names fill my head. Walter and I will fish all morning in Hotham *Sound*, then head home turning into Jervis *Inlet*. From the Inlet we pass the Skookumchuck *Narrows*. You don't want to be in the Narrows when the tide is coming in or going out; that's when they have the rapids there.

If we ever did go through the Narrows—and sometimes we would sleep in the boat so we could catch the early morning slack—past the Narrows the shores broaden out. The ocean is called Sechelt Inlet there and goes all the way to the town of Sechelt. If we bypass the Narrows and keep heading south, we are no longer in Jervis Inlet, but are now in the *channel* between the mainland and Nelson Island, that channel whose name I have to think about. I have to take a run at that name. Here goes. *Agamemnon.* It must be a Native name—so long and complicated.

5. There are other lands

Then right at the water line begins the bush: the dark evergreen forest heads up into the hills, carpeted with chest-deep ferns and thistles and salal, that pokes up through the slash from old logging shows. It drives Walter crazy, this country, he tells me.

"In the bush you can't see fifty feet in front of you," he says, "but out here on the water, what a relief. Like being back on the prairies. You can see for miles."

Walter could tell that the word, *prairies*, did not click with me.

"No mountains back there, Joey. Low rolling hills, miles and miles of them, till you get to the flat-as-a-pancake dead centre of the continent. In Saskatchewan a man can pee off his back porch, and while enjoying that simple act, scan the countryside for miles around. Here on the coast you can't see a bloody thing for the goddam hills and rocks and trees. Your neighbour a hundred feet away… he might as well be on Mars. A man has to get out on the water to properly get his bearings. The view opens up. You can see a boat coming an hour away."

No mountains: the idea gave me a creepy feeling. I thought for a while, eyeing the wheel that Walter turned and the dials that, as long as he kept watching them, would make the boat keep going.

"Prairies," I said.

"You've been there," Walter said.

"Huh."

"It's like out here on the water," he added. "The wind is in charge."

His words gave me a picture. Soft curvy hills, dry grass whispering with the wind, and the wind humming with the sounds of the bugs that live in the grass. Cowboys, sixguns slapping their thighs as they ride shining horses across the dry fields. At the top of a rise, they shade their eyes with their hands as they scan the horizon for their cattle, or for other cowboys, or danger coming.

"Out here, you know when it's going to storm," Walter said. "You see the rain coming. You get to know who's fishing the inlet, and where they come from and where they're going and how they're doing."

Soon he would throttle down and it would be time to pull up our next string. If we were lucky the traps would be full of prawns, scrabbling and scratching at the black mesh, and we would fill the live tank with cages and it would turn out to be a good day.

"You've been there," Walter said. "In fact, you're from back there. Before your accident you used to talk about it, Joey. You and your sister."

Sister. I let the word slide through me and slither along the deck and splash in the water and sink. If we were on the prairies, I thought, Walter and I would be setting our traps in the sky—we would hook them up to big balloons. We would ride our horses across the dry grass, our strings of traps soaring up behind us, and we would be hauling down full baskets, big black baskets full of chittering birds.

6. Low tide

This is the moment when I say *why am I doing this.*

Walter charges the *Medusa Deep* at the float. Don't be scared Joey say I, grabbing onto a guy line. Walter turns hard and cuts the engine and for a second everything stops. We hang there at the peak of our own wake, and then the boat surges toward the barrier of rubber tires.

I jump onto the dock first, to brace the boat by grabbing the gunwale to stop it crashing into the float. Then to tie it off, first one end then the other to the mooring rail. Walter taught me how to do this. It was not easy at first.

The guys in their white smocks grumble as they come down the steep ramp from the fish plant's dock. They come down the ramp, step by dainty step, holding onto the wooden rail because it is so steep. Each of them carries a two-wheeled dolly under his arm.

"Hope ya guys got no fish."

"Five hundred pounds. Maybe more," says Walter. Actually it hasn't been a great day and we have about 250.

"Can't you SOBs come at high tide?"

"We try," says Walter. He has explained to me that it is no use trying, not at this time of year. The high tide is at late night and late morning, when nobody is bringing in prawns.

I swing cages of prawns from the live tank onto the gunwale and the guys stack them on the dollies. They pull the loaded dollies up the ramp. As they near the top they go slower and slower. The job gets harder because the ramp, despite its tar shingles and wooden cleats, gets slippery from the water that drips from the cages. Each guy pulls himself up by the rail and creeps up the ramp one cleat at a time. It is a hard job, I know that from experience.

7. Rose

I start to drain the live tank and hose it out but Walter says why not come up, see your buddies. This is what he says to me every day, and I shake my head, furtively looking around for little tasks and chores that will keep me on the boat. Things to do that can't wait.

But he taps me on the shoulder. "Come on. We can finish up later."

We climb the ramp past the murmuring pump shed that sucks water out of the harbour and intrudes it up into the blue plastic totes that cover one side of the loading dock—the fish plant's live tanks, the hoses between them like throbbing veins full of the fresh seawater that the prawns need.

We cross the concrete pad of the loading dock and push through a barrier of plastic ribbons into the main room of the fish plant. Inside there is a crowd in white smocks and yellow rubber aprons and hairnets. Around the stainless steel fingerpacking tables they are mostly women.

I see a small woman in a white smock and jeans moving among them. She talks to everyone, telling them that they're doing this good, or they could do that better. When you see her out of the corner of your eye she looks like a young woman—she is slender, and there is an energy in how she moves—but she has short grey hair and I know it is Rose.

"Hello there handsome," she says.

"Hello yourself," says Walter.

"I wasn't talking to you." Rose turns towards the guys who are taking our cages off the dolly and stacking them on the scale. By now, enough water has drained out of the cages that the prawns are more frantic than ever—but without the weight of water, what the scale says will be closer to the truth. "Everything look kosher at this end?"

If a skipper has problems with the weight that Rose writes down, now is the time to speak up. She gets Walter to sign the sheet where she's written how many pounds of prawns we've brought in.

"Haven't seen you around here lately," she says to me.

"I stay down on the boat when we unload," I say. "Then I go straight home."

Rose catches me looking around the plant, at the faces of the people, and the figures in their smocks. "Don't worry," she says, "Jag's not here."

"I was just looking around."

"Joey, his bark is worse than his bite."

Actually, the flickering had started at the corners of my vision. I had looked over at Margaret, a fat pretty woman who faced me across the fingerpacking table, her eyes on the scattering of prawns in front of her, and beside Margaret was her daughter Iliana. I had seen snaking up for a half-second between the mother and her teenage girl, a tendril of blue fire.

"You all look real busy," I say. "We oughtta go."

"I don't let him intimidate me and I'm just a little old lady."

"Somehow," Walter says to Rose, "I never think of you in that way."

"Walter Conacher, I don't want to know how you think of me…"

Walter laughs.

"...an awful man like you," Rose says.

"You have circles around your eyes," I say.

Rose makes an exasperated sound. "I'm tired," she says. "You guys are bringing me too many prawns."

As we pull away from the dock Walter says, "Is that why you always come back to the dock with me? Does that Jagges intimidate you?"

I don't answer him.

"Because you could just get off at the plant and walk home or get a lift from there. You'd get home a lot faster."

"I guess so."

"Not that I mind giving you a ride."

I say nothing as we pass a cluster of little islands on our right. Beyond them I see Whiskey Slough.

"Danny Jagges was always a big loud piece of shit as a kid," says Walter. "I thought he'd mellowed out with age, but in recent years he has backslid. Business pressures, I dunno. That shit gets to all of us."

"I guess so."

The shoreline up ahead is a jumble of boats and docks and buildings. As we get closer I start to distinguish the boats at the government dock from the clutter of the Madeira Park shoreline.

"I don't suppose you want any advice about women," Walter says.

I am afraid to say no.

"When someone, I mean a woman, looks tired—and Rose always looks tired during prawn season because she works eighteen hours a day, seven days a week for two or three months—when a woman looks tired, it's much better to say something like, 'have they been keeping you up late, you poor thing?'"

"They?"

"Joey, it doesn't matter. It's what you say that makes the difference."

"Difference?"

Walter harrumphs. "I might as well talk to the depth sounder. Jeezus. You've got to be able to tease women, but let them know you really care. The more overt stuff, making cracks about bedroom eyes, implying they've been up all night screwing some guy, that's not my style. I don't go for that."

"Me neither."

"Simple. Gentle. Concerned. 'You look so sleepy'—that's a good one. 'Can I get you a coffee?' But telling a woman she's got circles around her eyes, that's not what she wants to hear."

We stop talking for a while, then Walter says, "Though I guess with you and Rose, well… you two can say what you want to each other."

We're getting close to the government dock in Madeira Park where Walter ties up for the night. "You don't know what I mean, do you?"

I head out to the deck and get ready for our approach and work my hard-earned skill to, at the last moment, jump onto the float and tie us up.

"I don't suppose you remember any of that."

This is way over my head, so I say nothing. "Damn though," Walter says, "That woman *does* look tired."

8. The magnificent creatures you see before us

Sometimes something weird comes up in the traps. It is an animal, but like a bud off a spider plant, it cradles itself inside its curled leaves. You would not think it was a sea creature.

Sometimes, after the traps are emptied, I leave one of these things on the sorting table. It is not something you would want to cook and eat, and it lies there wet with stinking bottom mud like it's dead and rotting. But it is not dead, it's thinking. From its soft cold mud, fifty or eighty fathoms down, it's been seized into this world of amazing heat. But I notice that the bottom creatures, these creatures are ready for anything. They don't show fear before their enemies.

If we leave it alone, gradually this little spider plant uncurls its brown leaves and props itself up on their pointed tips and starts to walk. It is hoping that if it keeps creeping along, it will reach the saltchuck again. Instead it reaches the edge of the table and stops. It has never been in this much light before, or touched a tabletop, or looked down such a long way through
air, to the deck under our feet.

I pick it up and again it curls into itself. I show Walter.

"I can believe," he says taking it from my hand, "that once we were all little sea creepers, and that some of us evolved into octopuses, and some of us crawled out of the water and turned into monkeys and then"—he held the little ball of mud up and talked to it "—into the magnificent creatures you see before us."

"But this—" he tossed it back to me and I caught it "—if you ask me, a million years ago a meteor musta splashed into Jervis Inlet and these things came crawling out. They've been down there at the bottom, never knowing where the hell they were, never breeding with the locals, never changing. It's an alien."

I wonder if that was true—that for years and years these things would stay down there on the bottom, and not change. Even if it is dark and silent down there, and cold so that each tiny creature hides inside itself a tiny furnace—such a heat you would never believe (I will tell you how I learned about this heat)—there are currents that push the creatures back and forth through the dark. They must always be on guard. The octopuses make themselves so thin the current cannot catch them, and through that undertow they slither like snakes to reach the holes or grottoes where they live. The wolf eels turn their heads into the current, and zig this way and that like sailboats against the wind, and the prawns flutter their thin little silky membranes or scrabble with their bony legs to find an anchor, some little weed or wire or toehold on the muddy bottom. If they don't watch out, a current will grab them and they will fly miles away, upswelling into the light or being drawn down, where it is so dark and cold and deep that even a prawn can't make a living there.

They hang on because if they don't, the world they live in will change. But the current keeps coming. The prawn hangs on, fighting the current, so that its life will not change. Meanwhile the mud and the muck it knows so well get swept away. New muck and new things, some living some dead, take their place.

So why hang on at all. I throw the spider plant thing over the side and we watch it hit the water. It spreads its leaves and begins its long happy fall, thinking it will land pretty much where it started. Not knowing anything different.

"I see no relationship whatsoever between those things and me," says Walter. "There's probably a market for them in Japan."

9. The name of a queen

She was born with the name of a queen, but everyone called her Sandy. From across the sales floor of Skookum Lumber, Alexandra Windebank saw the word sticking out like graffiti on a school bus. It was Saturday morning and the Vancouver office had declared a weekend sale, so there was a big paint display aimed at the cottage people.

Peinture.

"Sandy," said Chelsea, one of the high school girls. A man with a well-combed moustache and an immaculately shaved and polished head was leaning heavily on her counter. Two or three people were lined up behind him. "Can you check on a hold for this guy?"

"Step up to the service desk, sir," she called, "and someone up here can help you." She saw Chelsea frown and shrug: *I told him that.*

"I ordered it here," the man said, eyeing Chelsea hungrily. Sandy didn't recognize the guy, but she sure knew the type. Chelsea was young, plump and pretty with dyed-blonde hair and he was one of those guys who, if he could make her day miserable, it would be the start of a perfect weekend for him.

"If you can just come back here sir," Sandy said. "I'll make sure you get what you need."

Double entendre, plus the suggestion of special treatment proved irresistible. The moustache fell for it and Sandy left him standing in Fasteners, surrounded by bins of screws and nails while she took his name, figured out what he was supposed to have on hold and disappeared into the stockroom. As she turned right and took another door to double back into the store, around the corner where he couldn't see her, the word flashed across her retina again.

Peinture.

She took a deep breath and tried to think good thoughts about the guys she'd trained to do the merchandising. They try hard, they do a good job and most of the time, she recited, most of the time…

On a hook she found the sanding belts that the moustache wanted, scribbled his name on a HOLD tag and cut back through the stockroom, brandishing them before her. "They *just* came in…"

An hour later the morning rush died down. Sandy took a sip of coffee and scanned the rows of merchandise, her eyes finally resting on the pyramid of paint cans with the red SALE sign. Chelsea came up from the cash register,
idly dusting displays as she wandered among them.

"Thanks for helping me with that guy," she said to Sandy. "The way he looked at me. He freaked me out a bit."

"I liked his head," said Sandy. "So shiny. Like a big Smartie." They laughed.

Out on the floor, she put her coffee on the topmost can and crouched. Chelsea came up behind her. "I watched them stacking those up last night." She twirled the duster nervously.

Sandy said nothing. She concentrated on the pyramid of cans.

"Uh, they did a good job there." Chelsea kept her eyes on Sandy and chose her words carefully. "Didn't they?"

"I've told them time and time again." Sandy stretched the fingers of her left hand as far around the offending can as they would go and pressed her right hand against the front. "If this collapses girl, run for cover and notify…"

Next of kin. That did it. Like an assassin gripping her victim's head she winced and gave a savage twist. The pyramid trembled, ever so slightly, but nothing shifted. The faintest of ripples crossed the surface of Sandy's coffee.

"Wow," whispered Chelsea.

"If I told them once I told them a zillion times," said Sandy. "English side *out*."

10. You will be forgiven

Horking and sputtering, I broke the surface and splashed toward shore. Wherever I looked the shore was a wall of rock that went six or eight feet up from the water before leveling out. I swam uselessly along its base, feeling like a spider in a bathtub. In my layers of clothes it was getting harder and harder to keep my head above the water. I could hear the guys yelling at me from out on the boats.

I found a crack in the rock, stuck my hand in and made a fist. When I braced my feet against the underwater wall I felt the weight of the whole ocean pulling me back into the water. I grabbed with my other hand and then I was sprawled on top of the rocks, water spilling from my layers of clothes back down the rock face. The noise from the boats changed. Now they were hooting and whistling.

I looked back at the men on the boats. It dawned on me that I had just put an end to my prawn fishing career.

All the time I was escaping from the *Medusa Deep*, Walter and Felix had been keeping one eye on me and one on their headings. They kept their boats idling in a slow circle. They were in shallow water, four or five fathoms deep just before the mouth of the cove dropped off into bottomless channel, and they had to keep their eyes on the rocks and not let the ropes foul their props, and make sure they didn't collide, and make sure they didn't spill the huge pile of bones that hung between them like the bagged evidence of some awful crime. The skeleton in the nets turned and turned and slowly the empty sockets of the huge skull came into view. I shoved my way into the trees where I couldn't see it or be seen.

Walk back along the shore, I heard a voice in my head. *Along the shore to Felix's house.*

Meanwhile, my body pushed its way through the bush.

There will be dry clothes there. Walter will pick you up at the dock.

The ground was rough and through my wet socks I felt every root and thorn.

You will be forgiven. You can go back to being Walter's deckhand.

I kept plowing through the bush to get away from the shore. If I kept on in this direction, I would get to the highway—no way I could miss it. I would hitch a ride home. I would not have to face Felix, who had collected all his buddies together to raise the whale, or Walter, who I had just shafted real bad. Jumping ship in mid-season means you don't care whether or not the skipper is out there trying to pilot the boat, and also keep fishing, with no deckhand. A real insult.

My feet hurt. The branches whipped my face. Splashing into a stream made me gasp, but it made my feet hurt less, at least until I got back onto land. My way through the woods began to slope upwards. Soon the sounds from the shore disappeared and the ground got so steep that I was climbing more than walking.

At the summit of the hill a rock face rose above the trees. It wasn't as steep as the shore had been. Once I managed to climb it, I looked around, but this didn't help much. Everything looked so different.

I took off my clothes and laid them out to dry. I pulled stuff from my pockets. Rubber gloves, my pocket knife, bits of white pulp that used to be a Kleenex, a plastic prawn tag, a key, a loonie, two quarters, two dimes and two pennies, some kind of ID card, my name and address now washed off—and half a soda cracker which was now a sort of whitish paste not much different from the Kleenex. The afternoon sun was warm on the cliff top. I lay back on the moss to peel off my socks. It hurt where they were stuck to my feet with crusted blood. I lay my feet out under the sun.

Now I was ashamed.

Come prawn fishing with me, said Walter—*you'll make more money than at the plant. Maybe it'll—you know—do you some good.* He had given me a chance.

Everything else in my life was a mess. The ladies in the clinic saying *now Joey, use your words.* Christof at the lumberyard: *I know you're trying hard Joey, but we can't afford to have you banging up equipment and pissing off the customers.*

Finally at the fish plant I seemed to make some kind of headway. I was welcome back there every spring. Then Walter appeared at the door of my trailer and asked if he could come in. *Why don't I give you a try as a deckhand.* Standing warily in the midst of my cluttered kitchenette: *You better not treat my boat like this.*

The prawn fishing ate me up so that nothing was left for anything else, but that, by and large, was okay. The alarm went off at 4:30 a.m. I would walk in the fading dark to the fish plant and stand on the float until Walter came. At first he would dock, and briefly tie up so I could come aboard, but after a few days the *Medusa Deep* would just coast in dead slow, barely brushing the rubber bumpers. I would throw my knapsack onto the deck and jump after it, and then Walter would speed up, taking us out the mouth of the harbour—empty, so early, of other boats—and up the channel to the inlets, their green waters deep and churning with eager prawns. By 7:30 at night we would be back at the plant. At 9:30 I would be in my trailer falling asleep in front of the TV, then waking up at midnight moaning, the tendons in my hands on fire from the long day of pulling traps over and over, hundreds of times a day in and out of the cold underwater canyons.

Then one morning, instead of continuing up the channel, we turned in at Felix's oyster farm. Last year, Walter explained, there had been a great fuss because the corpse of a gray whale had drifted into the harbour. It was a menace to navigation. Some of the retired guys, always ready to form posses to get things done, had made great plans to blow it to shreds with dynamite—but before they could carry out their plan, Felix roped the carcass and for half a long day towed it up the channel to secure it in the little bay where he grew his oysters. He bored holes in it with a gas-powered auger and finally persuaded the whole disgusting swamp of bones and blubber to sink. He had plans for mounting and selling a whale skeleton, once he'd given the little creatures at the bottom of his bay a year or so to do their work.

"By now it should be nibbled clean. Skeletonized," Felix said aloud when we arrived, enjoying the feel of the word on his lips. He said it again as we unclipped the scotchmen from each end, attached our winches to the net and began hoisting the huge bundle from the bay's bottom. Slowly, muck and water drained off the huge mass like a raised shipwreck, the carcass as long as both our boats put together. My job was to stand on the gunwale of the *Medusa Deep* with a boat hook and push against Felix's boat to keep it safely away.

I felt proud that I could work with all these people around. I was, as they say, coming right along.

Then the deck shook as if the boat had been seized with a racking cough. I almost dropped my boathook. Felix had started a saltwater pump. He held a hose and as the pressure surged and grew, he began hosing silt from the bones. I saw him smile and his lips move as he said that new favourite word. I watched amazed to see this shapeless mass transform into white bones. It was magic.

But there was something else in there. I smelled smoke, looked back at Felix, and saw flames dancing around his feet as he gleefully blasted the huge corpse with the saltwater hose. I looked back and saw there on the skeleton, pearls of seawater flickering off its blackened chain, the head of a little carved wooden bird, hanging there from the whale's bones.

"Lookit that," someone said. Now I could see the flames around them all.

I looked again at the dangling bird. Then I let go of my rope. I ran across the deck. I put one boot on the gunwale and jumped into Agamemnon Channel.

I pumped my arms and legs for shore. I felt something under the water pulling at my feet and I thought of the hands of all the people who had gone into the water and not come out. My head went under, and I kicked to get back into air. *The Medusa Deep* was only a hundred feet from shore, but the water was so cold and my feet were so heavy that I started to go down. Then I felt the hands slip off one foot. Then the other. Glumly dropping my gumboots from their clammy hands, the soft, pale dead turned back sulking to the sea bottom.

11. Measuring heat

From behind the service desk, Sandy blinked hard to wake up. The morning's first customer, standing four feet in front of her, was tapping his fingers and staring off into a far corner.

She blinked again. *Blink. Ouch.* Like there was hot sand in there. Newly single, she liked to joke that without Greg in the bed, she slept like a log, but it was a bad joke and everyone knew it. In reality she was sleeping like shit and she looked like it. *Blink.* Dammit, the customer was still standing there.

"…measures temperature by reading ultraviolet light." He was still faceless, but she registered a trimmed beard and yellow floater coat. She gave up and let his voice and image swim into focus.

"Haven't seen such a thing."

"It's been on TV for weeks."

"We don't have it," she replied. "Maybe in town. Up here in the boonies, we haven't seen any such creature."

"Do you think you can order it in?"

One hour and ten minutes until her first break.

"Do you know who makes it?"

"How the hell should I know?" the customer said. "It's hardware. This is a hardware store."

Sandy sighed. "Let me take your number. I'll phone around and call you back. If I can find out anything about it."

She wrote his name and number on a scrap of paper from the counter tray. "It might be something they just have in the States," she warned.

The phone rang and still scribbling, Sandy reached out and grabbed it. "Skookum Lumber, Sandy speak…"

"I thought you were going to call me," her husband's voice said. "I thought we were going to get a lawyer…"

"It's pretty busy here."

"We have to start moving on," Greg said.

"Moving on," Sandy said. "In other words, selling my home out from under me so you can, what—take your girlfriend on a cruise? Buy her a big week in Vegas?"

"So," the thermometer guy said, "you'll call me when it's in?"

"Yes," Sandy said, holding her hand over the receiver. "Soon as I handle this call, I'll be tracking it down."

Greg, on the other end of the line, waited until he could tell she was done. "You don't hafta sell the house," he said, "You can buy my half off me."

"For years we've been scraping by with two incomes. Now you figure I can take out another, bigger, mortgage to pay all on my own."

"You're always so good with money."

Don't humiliate me with your goddam compliments. She said, "Joey's gone missing."

"Oh jeez," Greg said. "You finagled him into that trailer and he's still staying out all night?"

"He jumped off a boat. Up the channel."

"Oh jeez. You mean he's like, lost at sea?"

"He swam to shore and took off into the bush."

A chuckle. "What a frickin' guy. What got into his head?"

"He's been deckhanding for Walter Conacher. They were hauling up that whale that Felix sunk off his dock last year. It's just bones now, but something about it freaked him out. He took one look, jumped in the drink and took off into the trees. Yesterday."

"Jeez..." There was a silence at the end of the line. "I'm sure he'll turn up soon."

"He's been out in the bush all night."

"Sandy... I'm sure that bugger's fine."

"I haven't slept a wink."

"He'll turn up."

"Last night, every little noise... I thought it might be him, finding his way out of the bush and down the highway and trying to get in."

"There you go. Getting yourself all uptight over Joey again. Tonight take a Gravol, for Christ's sake. He's out of your life, out of our..."

"You were going to say 'out of our house,' weren't you? Hey, how's Ginny doing by the way?" She glanced up to see a bulky white-haired figure shoulder his way through the front door and head toward the service counter. Pat Cranshaw. I guess sooner or later, she thought, I've got to start acting civil and civilized.

On his end of the line down in Burnaby, Greg sighed. "Sandy. This is a business call."

"Not for me it isn't." She slammed the receiver back in its cradle and looked at what she had in her right hand. "It's personal," she said to no one in particular. In her hand was a slip of paper with a man's name on it, a phone number, and the words "measures temp."

"It's really fucking personal," she said out loud.

"What's that Sandy?" said Pat Cranshaw.

"Pat darlin'," she said. "What can I do ya for?" She crumpled the bit of paper and threw it in the blue bin. The phone rang. "Hang on a sec."

It was Christof. "Line one," he said. "It's about your brother."

12. The bush

This morning, walking to the dock at 5 a.m. the sun was full above the horizon but the air was cold. There was snow on the mountaintops that look down on the inlets.

"Watch out for the space heater," said Walter, when I jumped onto the *Medusa Deep* and joined him in the cabin. "Jesus Christ, here it is June."

"Here it is June," the lady in the supermarket had said, "and where's summer."

"Where's the summer," I said to the woman who came to my trailer, who claimed to make sure I wasn't piling stuff on the baseboard heaters, and I repeated the question, pestering her until she went away.

The summer started while I slept on the cliff top.

I stood up dizzy with the heat and almost stumbled over the edge. I backed away from the drop and looked down at myself. The skin down there was bright pink and did not feel too good. My clothes were dry but I dressed slowly because every weave of the fabric felt like a jagged metal edge against my skin.

From the cliff top I could see no boats on the channel, or Felix's place where we pulled up the bones. There were just treetops and a ribbon of water already darkening, the shadows of the trees creeping across its still surface.

I turned into the bush, trying to steer straight away from the channel and toward the highway. Out of the sunlight into shadow, like pushing down into cool water, the sounds of wind on the hilltop fading to discreet rustlings and twitterings that followed me through the thorns and thistles into the trees.

After the long climb from the water's edge I was now walking downhill. I began to get excited, stopping to listen for passing trucks, expecting any second to push through a gap and burst out onto the gravel shoulder. In minutes, happy to be thumbing a ride home.

But suddenly the ground fell away and I grabbed onto a fir branch to stop from falling. It was another rock face like the one I had climbed before.

I walked back and forth, rubbing fir pitch off my hands as I looked for a way down. But it seemed I was screwed—I couldn't find anything but cliff. Finally I came to an arbutus tree. From its roots, buried in the jumble of rock at the ridge's base, it snaked up the cliff and spread its leaves over my head. I took a deep breath and jumped onto its trunk.

I hit the tree hard. Its loose red bark exploded into flakes, and when I grabbed the trunk it was like scooping a handful of bees. Wrapping my legs around the trunk was worse. I used my legs like a big hand as best I could, shinnying down as slivers of bark ground through my jeans into my skin. The slick, knotted wood twisted between my legs. I hit a branch hard and lost my grip, grabbed onto something else, lost my grip again and fell into the crotch of the tree's biggest and lowest branch. I moaned, unwedged myself and dropped to the ground. My shirt and pants were ripped and through the rips I could feel the slivers like living things stinging and burrowing.

I stood up and Christ everything hurt. I turned and looked back up the cliff. Gotcha you bugger, I got down. I am here.

Sure you are down there asshole, but where are you?

True enough, the ridge was all I could see—a wall of rock in a sea of trees. But it still made sense that the ridge was between me and the water. If I walked away from the ridge, I would reach the highway. If I just kept walking I would get there. I would have to get there.

My body felt like it had been towed down a gravel road by a jeep. You wouldn't think it would be so hard, surviving in the woods, but it is. For example, there is nothing to eat. Sometimes in a clearing where the sun came through, I found blackberry vines. The thorns clawed at me as I passed, but there were no berries. Those come later in the full heat of summer, when the fish plant closes and the prawn boats are all tied up. That was weeks and weeks away. I was hungry and thought: I will be dead then.

My socks were ripped and my feet banged up. I took the rubber gloves from my jacket pockets and tried pulling them over my feet, but they slipped off when I tried to walk. So with my pocketknife I cut the sleeves off my jacket and tied them around my feet. I sliced them lengthways along the seams, then used what was left of my socks to tie each sleeve around an ankle. I stood up, took one step, then another. It was bad but better than it was before. I felt pretty proud.

Now the ground went downhill. I kept looking back at the cliff to get my bearings, until the cliff was gone in the trees. When I came to a stream I doused my face in the water and drank, then splashed through it and kept going.

All this time the woods were getting dark. I wanted to keep going anyway, and not stop, and find the highway and someone who would feed me and give me new socks and drive me back to where I lived. Then as it got darker and darker I whacked my shin on something, bounced off a tree trunk and fell on my ass.

I sat there trying to figure out how to keep going through the dark. While my brain was thinking, my body found an arbutus tree and started scooping fallen leaves with its hands. There were not that many leaves, and lots of them were damp with dirt and bugs. I lay down anyway. Heaped the leaves over myself, trying to use them for a blanket. Like everything else I had done that day, this arrangement totally sucked.

I lay in the dark and listened for encouraging sounds. The highway, I thought, must be very close. If I held my breath I would hear cars pass. If I stared hard enough into the darkness I would see headlights rippling through the trees. If I listened I might hear rescuers pounding the bushes, calling my name.

I looked, I listened. Nothing. I stuck up my head. The leaves fell away. I tried to scoop them back over me and the woods fell silent. I got up to pee, and when I was done I stumbled around for a long time until I found my pile of leaves again. I burrowed under the leaves with my hand until I felt a trace of the heat that my body had left in there. I lay down again. But it was a cold sleep, a scared sleep, a sleep where the night went on forever and I woke up again and again, opening my eyes wide for a hint of sunrise, not getting one, closing them.

13. My dream of the deeps

I dream that out in the cold inlets something has happened. Like an idiot, I have gone over the gunwale again and this time there is no nearby shore to swim to. This time I am sinking and there is nothing to stop me. The ocean has claimed me. No amount of squirming can loosen its hold.

Squirming and kicking until finally there is no reason to hurry. The growing darkness is no longer scary. When I reach out in the dark someone takes my hand. There is so much heat in that hand. I let go and the heat leaves a trail of light like an afterimage of fire. I shudder as the last of the heat drains out of my body.

On the inlet bottom the little things are drawn to the aroma of my blood and skin. Time passes. The current lifts me up. I am reborn in a cloud of plankton and worms and little fishes. They tear and burrow and nibble and the gasses bubble out through the holes, and then I sink. Down so deep that light means no more than the flickers of visible heat inside the bodies of the creatures that live down there. Up and down, light and dark, alive and dead—there is no difference any more.

Above me is the dim memory of a world so harsh and mean that I would never want to go back. Below me is the rich soft sea bottom—everything alive begins and ends down there. When I settle on the bottom, a cloud of muck and bones and hair, slowly dissolving into the salt current, the prawns know that I have come. They smell that I am there. One scuttles along the bottom and another follows, and then more, all pulled along by the excitement of the first, and soon I am mobbed by prawns, hopping along the ocean bottom from every direction like ants to a popsicle stick. As they dart and twitch and chew with their mandibles, an octopus comes to feed, then a wolf eel. Above them, the rainbow-edged fin of a prowling dogfish flickers in the dark.

Then I am pulled off the bottom, up faster and faster and right through that ceiling. Back into that withering immensity of light and space where from one second to the next everything changes. As if the first death was not bad enough, up in the light my bones will dry and crack, the delicious bits of gristle and marrow that the little prawns and crabs and roach clips love will flake and blow away in the wind. Everything in me strains to get back to the sea, but then my body breaks the surface. I have this dream so many nights.

14. The dead already raised

At night the sea cools and the creatures there stir and flutter their weary limbs.

The water's surface ripples and whirls at their distress and as the land cools in the night, the water draws its warmth back to the sea. From the shoreline, cool breezes enter the trees and snake upwards through the forest, staying close to the ragged ground. Up into the hills the ocean sends the breezes looking to caress the warm exposed shoulders of the rock.

All night I heard the breezes snickering in my ears as they peeled away the leaves covering my body and stole my heat back to the sea. I tried to cover myself again. Then I was too tired and just lay there trembling and whimpering. Again and again I closed my eyes and thought, when you wake up it will be daytime. Then I would open them and see nothing. Finally I closed my eyes and heard birds begin to call from the hilltops. The birds tell you when there is something coming, that there will be a change. Then I heard something force its way through the bush. I feared a bear or something worse—a cougar or a supernatural creature like a sasquatch or tsonqua that you would only see at a time like this. But I opened my eyes.

There was someone there. There was a woman leaning over me in the dark under the trees speaking to me, saying, "Joey? You should go home."

"*Home?*" I sat up with a rustle of dead leaves but she was gone, already pushing away from me through the firs. Shivering, I lay there watching and the outline of a grey sky seeped slowly out of the trees.

I pushed myself aching and slimy off the ground. Ahead of me, a shadow slipped away into the growing light, and a voice coughed and roared like a grizzly. The voice revved up into the sound of a motor. All this time, I thought, the highway has been right here. I pushed my way through the last of the bush.

I came out into a clearing that had been blasted out of the trees, its coarse gravel glowing grey with the dawn light. On my left a dirt road led off into the bush, overgrown with broom and scrub alder and blackberry. The other side of the clearing dropped off into the water. No boats were tied up to the slouching wooden dock, its floats and pilings peeling off into the bay.

My first step into the clearing was like walking onto a stage. I felt like everyone had their eyes on me. From the far side of the clearing a doe looked back over her shoulder and bounced silently into the bush. There was no one and nothing but echoes, but amid the echoes was a man's voice, calling my name.

I wobbled toward the ramp that led down to the dock.

I looked across the water. There was a boat out there.

"It's all been a big mistake," I said.

The boat was idling slowly toward the dock. It was the *Medusa Deep*, with Walter leaning off the deck helm. "Can you make it down to the float," he shouted. "Watch your step, it's falling apart."

Beyond his boat I could see Agamemnon Channel and across the channel Nelson Island. The wood of the dock was punky and full of holes and the ramp was steep. I tried to walk down it and almost fell. I was stiff as a zombie and goddammit my feet hurt. I turned around and backed down, holding onto the rail, the way old people go down ramps at low tide. The rail rattled and groaned. I walked backwards, looking at the footprints I was leaving in the dry old wood, smudges of mud from the forest mixed with blood.

When I made it onto the float, the ghosts were gone and all I could hear was the engine of the *Medusa Deep*. I watched as Walter guided the boat in dead slow, on the lookout for half-sunk timbers or loose cables. I wondered if he might have any food on board.

15. The ghosts

"You might not want to watch this."

Sandy knew that Flo was giving her mere seconds to respond. She sneaked a glance at the man on the gurney's feet.

"Joey," she gasped. "What the hell?"

"Toldja," said Flo.

"I got scared," said Joey. "I was on the boat, and I got scared and jumped over the side."

"You can't just go jumping into the water," Flo teased. "This isn't Jamaica, you know. The water's cold."

"My boots fell off," he explained. "But it was just the water sucked them off." He yelped.

Sandy had to look away. Flo began swabbing Joey's feet from a pink bottle. She was a large grey-haired woman in hospital greens who, as she worked, cooed a steady stream of comforting sound about X-rays—should they or shouldn't they—were there broken bones—she didn't think so—no matter what, she was sure it would be all right.

"When we went to Jamaica two—no, three—Easters ago, we went swimming every day. In the ocean. It was so clear you wouldn't believe it."

"They just filled up with water," Joey said, his voice tense with pain. "Ouch. Really. Nobody pulled them off. Ouch. Aii."

"When do you think he can go home?" Sandy asked, wishing that she could get out of here and that somehow Flo would volunteer to keep this up overnight, the swabbing and the cooing, maybe even for days.

"Just let me put on a proper dressing," Flo said, "and you two can tapdance out the door together."

Sandy walked back up to Skookum Lumber to get her car. She knew she should check in with Christof at the store, but everyone would start yapping: how's Joey, did he have hypothermia, had he totally relapsed and was once again crazy, was he going to die, et cetera. Dreading that, Sandy walked directly to her car looking straight ahead and greeting no one. Sure the store was busy and Christoph needed her—so what. Basically the world works so that the good guys—like Christoph, old Pat Cranshaw, that's all she could think of for now—get pushed aside and shafted, while self-centered pricks such as Greg—and in conjuring his name she thought for the first time, *good riddance*—and her big brother Joseph, gorgeous Joe the good time boy, now Joey the Harbour's favourite village idiot—can take up all of our time with asshole antics and stunts and bailing just when people need them the most.

But he was her brother. There was no severing him off. But was he going to take over her life? Her life, as it was, was bad enough, but she was used to it. The normal everyday edge-of-doom state of mind, fretting over every mortgage payment and hike in car insurance, paying the hydro bill with the credit card, trying and failing then trying again.

It would not take much to slide into squalor—in fact Sandy was afraid it would only take two steps. Step number one had been taken: not having Greg around to help with the mortgage. Step number two: Joey, freshly reclaimed from invalid status, sliding back into it again. Next she would be explaining to him why they were closing up the trailer and selling it so he could move in with her (or, to torture herself even more, why not fantasize selling the house and building a miserable room onto the trailer so she could move in there—why not?).

Meanwhile, prospects of a half-decent marriage, babies, picnics, a dependable car, any kind of humdrum half-assed middle-class life were all down the tubes. In thirty years Sandy and Joey would be a prematurely-ancient couple nobody much saw or discussed. The nadir of coast living. She'd seen it happen. A satellite dish thrusting out of a wall of thorns.

When she pulled up in front of the clinic, Flo was waiting there with Joey in a wheelchair. Sandy got out of the car and slammed the door. She wanted to rattle away at Flo, as they coaxed Joey into the passenger seat. *It's just like when I first picked him up from the hospital. Arden gone, and him a wreck, and no one else to look out for him—*

But all she actually said was, "He doesn't need that, does he?"

"He's got to keep off his feet," Flo said, "at least for a few days."

—and all of us kept on waiting for Arden to come back, and she didn't, and for Joey to recover and get back to normal, and he didn't—

"Once you get him home, he goes nowhere."

All Sandy could do was hiss, and Flo turned away to concentrate on Joey. "Raise your arm."

"No," said Joey.

"You're as bad as your sister." Flo clucked and raised Joey's arm and reached around his torso. "They'd fry my rear end, if anyone found out I let you drive away without a seatbelt." The seatbelt clicked. Flo stood back.

—and Arden was gone, little white Toyota and all, never to be heard from again, never to call or write, never to appear as a new contact in my inbox, never to come clean and admit, I lured your brother up that old logging road and beat him with an axe handle—

"If you can bring him back in tomorrow…" Flo said.

—or shoved him off a cliff and left him for dead because just one time too many he'd maxed out the credit card or stayed out all night or come home drunk with Walter and the guys in the band—

"…we'll have another look at those feet and change those dressings."

—but Sandy had already slammed the door, was backing out onto the road. She went heavy on the gas and the brake and took the peninsula's curves at top speed, biting her lip not to grin when Joey moaned and braced himself against the pressure on his wounds and sores.

She insisted on helping him totter on crutches onto the porch of his trailer. Then, tugging his arm from her vicelike grip—after all, she reflected, he was a pretty strong SOB—Joey dug through his pockets. He had lost his boots in the water and since the accident two years ago she hadn't seen his wallet, and he still didn't have a new one. However, somehow after jumping off Walter's boat he still had his pocketknife and door key. It took him a few minutes to get the key in the lock and make the door open and for those minutes Sandy hovered inches away, grinding her teeth and twitching to take over, watchful and buzzing like a hungry mosquito.

As usual, Joey's place looked as if it had been ransacked by burglars. Sandy sat him down on a stained armchair and got him a can of pop. For a few minutes she picked up stuff out of the fridge and sniffed at it, dropping it in the garbage or putting it back. The bacon she sniffed twice and decided to take a chance. She threw together bacon and eggs and turned away to clean up while he devoured it.

She was surprised to see the bed already made. Joey explained that *make the bed every morning* was one thing the ladies at the hospital had managed to drill into him. Seeing the bed like that made Sandy feel less like murder. As soon as he was finished eating, she grabbed his plate and cutlery.

Drying dishes she heard him say, *go home.*

He had turned on the TV, leaning back in the armchair with his feet up on a plastic milk crate.

"Believe me I will," she said. "Soon as I…"

"It was the ghost who said that," Joey explained. "She woke me up and I followed her to where it was light. 'Go home,' she said. 'You don't need these people!'"

"I don't know what you're talking about."

"Whenever I try to get somewhere," Joey said. "I just run into ghosts."

16. The woman who is so unhappy

And so they ended, my dreams of being a fisherman, leaving me with the woman who is so unhappy and curses me for her unhappiness.

Yes, we are together again. Sitting alone in my trailer, when I hear the crunch of my driveway beneath her car tires I make a whimpering noise. I move someplace where I will look busy when she pushes through the side door.

"Dammit, keep off your feet." I'm not hard to convince.

For the first couple of days I was sleepy and, when she wasn't there, I would get around the trailer on my hands and knees. One afternoon hitting my head on the bathroom door, closing my eyes and waking up when it was dark outside.

Then the trips to the clinic stopped, and the woman would change the bandages herself when she came to the trailer. My feet were quickly healing: "They are pretty much filling in," she admitted. I thought of salt mud silting into the cuts, preparing my feet for the day the ocean bottom claims me.

But all this time I was angry with myself. By turning my back on the fish plant and going out fishing with Walter I had blown it.

I told the woman I would need gumboots so I could go back to the plant, and the next day she brought me a pair, though she pointed out, "Of course, the plant has pretty well done all its hiring for the season."

"I'll go down there and ask Rose," I said, looking at the socks she had brought.

"…and there's not much of the season left."

I twirled the socks around.

"You have to take the labels off," she said. She tried to snatch the socks away from me but I held on. I went to the kitchen drawer and found scissors to cut the labels.

"And the staples," she added. I said yes, right, and I worked at prying them out with the tip of the scissors. The woman plopped down at my kitchen table and just sat there looking at me, wringing her hands.

Finally I stood up in my new boots and socks. "These feel good."

"Don't sleep in them."

"No way." But I thought of the great stuff that I could do now.

"And don't think you're ready to go out hitting up Rose for a job or anyone else. You're not ready to work anywhere."

"I'm fine."

"Your feet must hurt like hell."

"They're fine."

"If you try to spend any time on them, those cuts will open up. You'll undo all the work I've done."

"I might walk down to the plant right now."

She crossed her arms. "Go right ahead."

"You have to go, right?"

She looked at her watch. "No hurry."

I was hoping she would leave so I could back down from what I had just said. Already, after a minute standing around in gumboots looking ready for action, my feet were feeling tender.

"Okay," I said, heading for the door.

On the steepest part of the hill there was more pain than I expected. By the time I got to Francis Peninsula Road it was bad.

I did not know what to do. It was a long walk to the fish plant. I sat down on the bench in the school bus shelter.

After a few minutes the woman's car came down the hill. She gave me a quick glance and then pulled out onto Francis Peninsula Road. I could hear the car turning around down there. Then the car came back and stopped in front of the bus shelter. The woman left the engine running and got out.

"Get in the car!" she said, as I wobbled to my feet and started to explain my situation.

We drove up the hill. "I get sick of this bullshit," she said.

17. The women in their secret world

She left, complaining as always I'd made her late for work, leaving behind the smell of food and some sort of noodle thing on the table. I told her, trembling and humiliated, that from now on I could change the bandages myself. Then she wouldn't have to come and do it.

"That's okay," she said. "I don't mind." And then she was gone.

This will sound stupid, but this is a real feeling I have gotten from the women around me. All women know things that men do not know and—don't even think about it—things we will never know.

Rose herself is a good example of this. At first I didn't see her as someone who was on my side. We met for the first time at the fish plant when I was delivering bags of cement from the lumberyard. Something about her made me look away and try to remember if I knew her or had seen her before. All the time she was doing business and making jokes with the driver she was sneaking looks at me. When I caught her at this and our eyes met, quickly I would look at the wall.

Later, when I was looking at a bag of cement that I had dropped in a puddle, and the powder was mixing with the water in the puddle, and everyone was talking about cleaning it up before it started to set, and there was some talk about using the pump to pump it all up and sluice it down the bank into the water, and the driver had gone to get a snow shovel to scrape up the cement, and I was looking at the cement wondering what to do, I looked at Rose and her gray hair and asked her if she was, by any chance, my mother.

"I am eight years your senior, Joseph Windebank," she said.

The driver came back and put the shovel in my hand. "Now you scrape this stuff into these garbage bags," Rose added, "before we need a jackhammer to clean it up."

Rose didn't talk to me again for a long time and it occurred to me that perhaps my "mother" question had been a bad one. I was afraid to ask how she knew my age, or thought she knew it. After the lumberyard job had broken up into tears and insults, I went to the fish plant to apply for a job and was surprised to see that she was doing the hiring. If only I had remembered, I thought. But she hired me right away, having for some reason forgiven me.

Rose has a look, as Walter says, that catches your eye. When she walks by you might turn your head, thinking it's a slender young girl but no it's Rose, grayer and sharper around the edges than a young girl and giving you back a hard, forward look. Whatcha think you're looking at mister?

One Friday night at the Legion, her old man went to the john, Rose came out to the smokers' tent and pulled out a cigarette. By the time she blew her first smoke ring, a couple of guys had sat down with her to shoot the breeze. In fact one of them was Walter, who had brought me to the Legion in the first place. Later I mentioned to him that when he took off to join Rose, I was left sitting there in the smokers' tent with nobody to talk to.

"That is some lady," he said. "I've known her since she and Don first moved up here. Their kids were just little then, and that Rose was…" he took his beer and cradled it in his hands. "… I've always thought she was something else, that woman …" Then he gave me a look. "Are you having me on, Joey?"

Rose's husband Don is a good guy, big and slow like some of the young guys at the plant, but even older than Rose. Rose told me once that she and Don have been together so long that they hardly even have to speak, and I understand that in fact, after all these years, not much is spoken.

18. You should just come

The owner was up from the city when Sandy got back to Skookum Lumber. Mr. Prahzash was a burly grey-haired man whom everyone, at his insistence, called Chuck. When she showed up, hurried, worried and pissed-off from taking Joey home, Christof and everyone at the service desk fussed over her and made much of Joey and his condition. Chuck joined in. Chuck insisted that the wheels of Skookum Lumber turned on a foundation of mutual goodwill.

"Joey," he said. "That's your brother—the one who had the tragic accident?"

"Yes that's him," Sandy said. "He just had another tragic accident."

"…we tried him here for a time…" Chuck continued, "… but he decided to move on…"

"That's Joey all right. He's been deckhanding for one of our customers… a prawn boat."

"Ah," replied Chuck. "Commercial fishing. Sure boosts the local economy doesn't it."

A tense silence fell over the service desk.

"…and he likes that?"

"Oh just fine," said Sandy. "Though as of today I suspect he's decided to move on from that job too."

Everyone laughed and in the blink of an eye so did Chuck. In Joey's short career with Skookum Lumber, under supervision he had proven okay with hand-loading lumber into customers' vehicles. He was developing some skill with handling heavy sheets of plywood or drywall. But drawing on some inexplicable well of ambition, Joey had once, in an unsupervised moment, decided to transfer these skills to the yard's forklift and had sideswiped a customer's pickup before toppling a pile of one-by-four and driving a tine of the forklift deep into the cinder-block wall of the rental shop. By Skookum standards this was a forgivable sin, as was the tantrum he threw when he got off the forklift, swearing, crying and calling his co-workers, the Ford owner and various onlookers, assholes. But when he committed all these sins at once, Christof fired him on the spot, and everyone including Sandy—did she need the pressure, did she need the worry, the responsibility?—was relieved to see Joey go.

It was the name thing that burned her the worst. When he first got out of the hospital, and moved in with her and Greg, he was still pretty hopeless. But within a few weeks at Skookum he was calling the other yard guys by their names, and by the time the disability payments started coming and she set him up in his own trailer, Joey seemed, if not a friend and equal with Greg and his Legion buddies, then at least adopted by them as a kind of mascot when Greg would drive him down there for get-togethers.

"Now remember, his name is Greg and I'm Sandy. I'm your sister Sandy, you remember." But though he was quick to say "Greg," even when he was panting for approval, he could not say her name.

Greg was a lot more patient—gee, Sandy thought, I just remembered something good about him—and instituted his own program of therapy that included taking Joseph out to the Legion for the Wednesday hump night.

He made her feel like a substitute teacher snubbed by a schoolboy. On her good days, she wondered if maybe this made her special—that there was still a brother-and-sister relationship there, with all its sharp points and jagged edges. But most of the time, Sandy just wanted to take Joey by the shoulders and shake him and shout *Say it. Say it you prick. My name.* But she never once did that or anything remotely like it.

At home she pulled out a photo album. In the early pictures she and Joey were kids, mugging beside snowmen, sprawling in front of Christmas trees, in swimsuits on the shores of Emma Lake. Saskatchewan—they had real winters there, that's for sure. There was her first job, in Dad's hardware store, Sandy smiling and Dad beside her assuming a proud expression—now she knew what it must have been like for him, why he joked and fidgeted and was off to the front counter as soon as the flash faded.

Her brother had been a shy boy, but he eventually managed to work his personality to best effect. By the time he was old enough to go out to work, he had ways of staying on good terms both with bosses, who wanted a kid who got the job done and didn't say fuck in front of the customers, and with his co-workers. Guys his own age, ordinarily afraid not to be caught swearing, spitting and goofing off in front of their peers, seemed to find in his easygoing nature an excuse to show their better sides.

Joey met Arden in his second year of humanities studies at university in the city and soon brought her home for a weekend.

After Sunday dinner, his family had waved goodbye when the couple drove away in Joey's rusting Datsun pickup.

"I don't know if she's the girl for him," Sandy's mother had said.

"I liked her," said Sandy.

"Bit of a hippie," said her dad.

"She's in fine arts," Sandy said. "She showed me pictures of her stuff."

Sandy, still in high school, was completely smitten with Arden, who seemed funny, beautiful, stylish—in a 1980s hippie sort of way—smart, warm yet sophisticated—all the things that Sandy would have liked to be, if only at home or at school or in the town or in the countryside around where she grew up, had she found anywhere a clue as to how to begin.

"I just hope," said her mother, "that once Joseph gets this arts degree, he decides to go into teaching."

Her husband made a dismissive grunt. "What else is he going to do?"

As if to show them, Joseph didn't go into teaching. Instead he made a meagre living doing this and that on the fringes of Saskatoon's tiny art scene. He and Arden moved in together, and visiting them once, Sandy learned how to silkscreen pictures onto cloth.

Then suddenly, they were on the west coast, in a spot on the map no one had heard of. "You should just *come*!" Joseph said on the phone. "You'll just totally dig it! Bring Greg!"

In fact, Sandy wasn't that sure about Greg, but Greg was all gung-ho for the BC idea. It took years for Sandy to get used to the misgivings she felt as they drove west for the first time. She sensed bad news as soon as the Rockies came into view. Mountains made her nervous, the way they *loomed*. She always felt like a storm was coming.

Soon Greg was getting work in construction—Sandy looked around for office jobs and finally got on as a cashier at Skookum Lumber.

"Hardware…" she could hear her dad's voice on the phone, "it's deep in the Windebank chromosomes, I guess."

"It's a job"

"Is Greg working?" he said, as if this would solve everything.

"Work is spotty out here," she said. "Hardly anyone works full-time at anything."

"Worse than the darn farmers back here," he said, and the course of the conversation was set. How while other people wintered in Texas or got laid off on EI or taught school and took the summers off, retail people would abide—opening the store at seven a.m., working Boxing Day, taking shit from friend and stranger alike, all to fuel the engines of the western economy.

"Yeah dad," she would say. "I guess so."

19. Zero: his triumphant return

Once I could walk without too much of a limp, I went to the plant. I spent all day putting it off, watched TV until I was too bored, then after supper I put on the boots and heavy socks. From the trailer it takes me a half hour to walk down the peninsula to where a side road drops down to the fish plant.

On my way down the hill to the plant I passed a bunch of young guys, hooting and yodeling as they loped and jumped and punched and pushed each other, coming up the hill to the parking lot.

I knew some of them by name and said hey and it turns out Rose had just canned them, every last one.

"She doesn't like our attitude."

"Fucking bitch."

"The job sucks." Kyle, a fat kid, had done halibut last summer and made four thousand dollars in three weeks. He was going to blow this shitstand and do halibut again.

"I want to see if I can work here," I said. Everyone laughed. Then someone called out Jag.

"Jag!" They started to scatter into the grass around the parking lot. "Jag!" They hid in the bush and behind cars. Like seagulls in the fog, their cries clattered off the hills and over the water. They cried together like gulls and then hushed up. Then I could hear it too. Shaking the rocks with its sound, a big silver pickup rumbled off the road and down the hill.

Wherever you went around Pender Harbour you would hear Jag's truck sooner or later. It had a big engine, a diesel they said, and whenever Jag made a stopover he would leave that diesel idling. If he was parked in front of a store, the plate glass windows would shimmer and shudder and keep shuddering until Jag got back in his truck, slammed the door and drove off.

I stood to one side as the light grew at the peak of the hill and then the nose of his truck broke the surface and the whole thing came into our view and started down toward the plant. There was no sign that he saw me—everyone else was hiding—except that maybe the truck's brake lights flickered once as he went past, then he kept on rolling down the hill.

The young guys came out of hiding. They looked down the road at the flash of Jag's taillights as he braked and turned at the water's edge.

"He'll be pissed."

I walked down the hill as they crowded into their old cars and trucks and one by one rattled out of the parking lot until it was empty. I looked back over my shoulder and only one person was left of the crowd, standing at the edge of the lot looking down at the plant. It was Kyle, the big blond kid with a sad face. He was just standing there, his shoulders slumped, then step by step he came after me, starting back down the hill. When I reached the wooden stairs that go up the side of the plant to the office I looked back and he had almost caught up with me, going faster now, head down, like a guilty dog.

Upstairs at the plant is mostly one big L-shaped room. In the far corner is a store room that is mostly locked, side by side with the ice room. In the other corner is the counter that separates the office where Rose does her work from the rest of the upstairs: the tables and benches where we sit to eat, the fridge and the sink and the microwave, the laundry corner with its piles of smocks and gumboots.

But there was no one there. Everyone who still had a job was down in the main room of the plant. Down there the radio was blaring 100.3 the Q, the long rollers of the sorter were turning, water was sloshing everywhere. The girls at the long stainless steel table were fingerpacking, but there were only four or five of them. They had lots of room—the table is long and wide and normally fingerpackers stood shoulder to shoulder along both sides and at each end.

In the middle of all this, Jag was yelling at Rose and she was yelling back. She was waving a prawn in his face, I'd say it was an XL—not only extra large, but extra crushed and shapeless, bits of leg and feelers dropping off as Rose shook it. It was too squished even to give away as an employee bonus.

"First busy day we've had in two weeks," he roared, "and you fire half the goddam crew."

"Playing Frisbee with the product," she yelled back, waving the squished prawn.

"They were getting the product *out*." Jag yelled.

"...smokin' dope in the john."

"Who's gonna get it out now?"

I said, "Uh Rose..."

Neither of them had looked at me so far, but as soon as I said that—not that anyone could hear above the racket in the place—Rose pointed, still without looking at me, she looked Jag straight in the eye and pointed right at where I was standing and said to Jag, "Thank God, we've got our Zero back."

"WHAT! You can't hire *him*."

"Joey does what you tell him. He's a good fingerpacker. A few more like him and a lot less of these coneheads and then we'll move some product."

Rose turned her back on Jag and came up close to me so she didn't have to shout. "I may live to regret this," she said, "but right now I'm glad to see anyone who's more or less grown up." Some of the girls on the floor made faces at her—as if I couldn't see them—and Rose frowned back. She shoved a hairnet at me. "Put this on and go upstairs and get a smock—remember, you're a Large—and get some gloves—d'you remember which box it is?—also Large, the box with the L. I see you got your gumboots already."

"My feet are way better."

Rose turned back to Jag. Jag looked away and said something I couldn't hear. He came toward me. I gripped the corner of the table. I couldn't back up without running into the girls who were fingerpacking. I was afraid he was going to hit me or kick me, and I thought maybe I could swing under the table and scramble towards the door. Then his arm shot out and Jag patted my shoulder hard. "Welcome aboard Joey," he said, "Glad to have ya."

"Can I have my old number back?"

"You got it," Rose said.

Jag said, "What's he on about?"

"The first hire every year is employee number zero. We lost our Zero tonight. Joey was our Zero last year and the year before and he would've been our Zero this year if Walter hadn't taken him out fishing."

Jag waved at the blonde kid who was moping around near the door. "What about this loser?"

Rose sighed. "He's as culpable as the rest of them."

Jag went up to the kid who, like me, backed up a step or two but stood his ground. They talked, but in all the noise of the big room I couldn't hear them. Rose took me past them, upstairs where she filled out a form for me and steered me to the dryer, where she pulled out a bundle of white smocks.

I was buttoning up when Jag came upstairs. "Kyle says he'll be good," he told Rose. He shot me a glance and went back down, and a minute later I heard the door of his truck slam. Rose took me downstairs where she got me some latex gloves. I felt the warmth of her body as she reached up and snapped the rubber band of the hairnet onto my head. This was all stuff I could do by myself and I didn't know why she was doing it for me.

"Not cut out for the life of a fisherman," she said.

"I did all right at first," I said. "Then one day…"

"You stay here with us on the dry land," she said. "We're glad to have our Zero back."

Because I'm taller she had to lean against me to fit the hairnet. I heard the roar of Jag's truck heading up the hill. Rose turned and headed out the door and down the stairs. Maybe this would work out, I thought.

20. The eager boats

Prawn season is the bridge between herring, that starts in early spring, and salmon and halibut in the summer. The government dock in Madeira Park is quiet September to spring, but come April fish boats are filling all the moorages, rafting up with buddies or tying up at the sport-boat float, pissing off the first of the summer tourists. Every other day the freezer guy from Sechelt has his van out on the dock to work on someone's freezer or live tank. When boats are late he stomps up and down the floats double-checking the boat names, shouting for the skipper and hissing swear words in German. Come the first days of May the sun is warming the wood of the floats, but the wind is still cold. The wind makes the prawn boats strain at their ropes, the ropes stretching and squawking, they are eager for the new season. Some of the boats have new coats of paint. Every day, their decks are more and more crowded with stacks of black-netted traps ready for the opening.

21. Springtime in the Legion

After all these years driving Madeira Park Road, Sandy barely had to slow down to see who was in the Legion. A stretch of the road overlooked the parking lot, and any long-time resident needed only a quick scan to know who was parked there.

That got harder as summer advanced. The winter regulars got busy, spring cleaning and fixing their boats and hardware and buying rain gear and supplies and making runs into the city. They were replaced by others, others who have been indoors all winter, scarfing down potato chips and Prozac, watching the satellite and listening to the police scanner, but now they too were cleaning and fixing and running up a tab at Skookum Lumber and stopping at the Legion for the lunch special or a beer after a hard day.

After work on Friday, Sandy drove to the Legion, but buzzed past it again and again like a nervous mosquito. She wanted to talk to Walter Conacher about Joey; she had it on good authority that he would be at the Legion with the oyster farmers on Friday, but she hadn't been to the Legion since Greg left and now she was scared to stop and go inside.

Besides drinking, the main attraction in any bar is the front door and who comes through it. Sandy was deathly scared that when she walked in, all eyes would turn to her and a thrill would run through the crowd.

Look there's Sandy Jacobs—here without Greg. Didja hear about Greg, didja?

If ya ask me, she's better off.

Didja see the ass on that Ginny—ya ask me, HE'S better off!

Sandy can be a real bitch. Get a few dollars behind on yer account...

And they would look away, shaking their heads.

Also, the Legion was the last place she had seen Joseph before his accident. In the parking lot, after an evening of draft beers, she and Greg had exchanged the usual wobbly heartfelt goodbyes with him and Arden, just like any other night. And then they were both gone forever. A week later, she'd been called to his hospital bed in Sechelt. She had followed her first impulse, trying to make eye contact—he blinked and spluttered and looked everywhere but at her—gripping his cold hand and telling him they would do anything to make him better.

Sometimes, hating herself, she wished that night at the Legion had been the last time. What if he had just got in the car and driven off and disappeared? So simple. What if Sandy had never laid eyes on him ever again? Her life would be so simple, it would be beautiful.

22. The fingerpackers

Six of us stand shoulder to shoulder along four sides of the stainless steel finger-packing table. A net bag gets upended and we start grabbing and packing the wiggling prawns that spill out over the table. The grading machine, that's built to sort them according to size, does its job with a high degree of imperfection. Inside each bag, all the prawns are supposed to be the same size. You can check how big a prawn is with plastic calipers, but with a bit of experience, a good finger packer can eyeball whether a prawn is undersize, medium, large, extra large, extra extra large or jumbo. You count them as you line them up in the box.

Everyone wears white hairnets and latex gloves, and yellow rubber aprons over their white smocks, and gumboots with heavy socks, and we stand at that table for hours every night. The season starts out half and half women and men and by the end it's mostly women, as one by one the men—except for me and Duncan—start leaving early or hurt their backs or get other jobs or get sent up the hill for being screwups, or just stop showing up.

Standing on rubber mats, all night the fingerpackers scoop prawns off the table, count them as they pack them into one-kg cartons, stack the cartons beside the scale. Prawns that get damaged or are otherwise no good get tailed. You tail them like this: taking a still-wiggly prawn in both hands, fit your thumb tips under the edge of its shell and then all of a sudden pinch the pink meaty tail off the head and legs.

Late in the shift the fingerpackers start to groan when they move and some of them stretch and do tiptoes in their rubber boots as their muscles cramp and their hands and shoulders seize up. But work is hard to come by up here so people will put up with a lot. And it being the fishing industry, when fall comes there is the pogey.

A boom box is in the corner. At one point, some young guys were bringing in their rap CDs but that got quickly shut down by popular demand. The night I arrived, Rose confiscated all the leftover CDs and put them up in the office. Mostly we listen to Q One Hundred Point Three, Island Rock from Victoria. In this big room with the noise of the hoses, freshwater and saltwater, the waterfall of prawns down the big rollers, the electric motor that turns the rollers on the grader, everyone talking and all the sound echoing off the concrete floor and walls, the ribbon doors open to the night, the radio just makes a big bashing racket but sometimes a part of a song will come through. There is a woman who sings "four million people surround us." That is one of my favourites, as well as "with arms wide open, under the sunrise." "Ev-er-y-thing's gonna be all right." "I'm like a bird," and so on. "Take it on the other side." What with noise and being busy I listen to these songs all season, but I never get any idea of what the names are, of who is singing them.

23. The road to Revenant Bay

What is that music? Sandy asked herself, as a flurry of melody came to her on the wind. Waiting at the dock to catch Walter on the way back to his boat, she got bored listening to the car radio and walked down to the floats. As well as music, the grumble of boat motors, mewing gulls, doors slamming, the wind carried voices from across the harbour, and sometimes her head would turn because a voice sounded familiar or, she thought, called her name. Soon it would be high summer and the harbour would be dotted with white yachts and none of the voices would be familiar and the bits of wind-chatter would be about cocktails and barbecues and when the store closed. The biggest of the yachts would sit anchored safely offshore, voices muffled by the hum of soundproofed gensets, faces invisible behind tinted windows.

But here was Walter's boat, and there was another boat rafted onto it, a wooden gillnetter just as old.

Sandy climbed onto the deck of the *Medusa Deep* and looked at the cabin door. What am I doing? she thought. If Walter were here, the door would be open. She tried it anyway. It was locked. A big man with close-cropped white hair came up out of the gillnetter that was rafted on to the *Medusa Deep*.

"Sandy," the man said, "Walter's up at the pub."

"Pat." Sandy looked at the name on the gillnetter. Sure enough, it was the *Muddy Waters*. Pat Cranshaw's boat.

As if she hadn't understood him, Pat repeated. "You can catch Walter up at the Legion. He's up there with the oyster guys."

Sandy looked down at her red polyester Skookum Lumber blazer, her neat slacks and permanent press yellow blouse. Oyster farmers tended to dress in stained yellow rain gear and black gumboots over varicoloured layers of wool, cotton and fleece. Among them she would feel like a schoolmarm captured by pirates or worse yet, like a boring little clerk who sold hardware for an hourly wage captured by pirates. "I don't feel like I'm dressed for that crowd."

"Why don't you come and have a visit with me," he said, "if you want to wait."

Suddenly she was sitting in the cabin of the *Muddy Waters* and Pat was handing her a shot glass of something.

"I hear that your brother went missing again."

"I got him back," she said.

"He's okay, I hope."

Sandy sighed. "Jumped off boat, swam to shore. Wandered the bush all night in sock feet. Did not die of exposure. Got rescued, feet patched up, now back at the fish plant packing prawns. Pat…"

Pat raised his eyebrows.

"…I wonder if you could tell me, just one more time, how you came to find Joey. The first time. Back when he and Arden went missing. The whole thing is still a big mystery to me."

Pat shook his head in dismay.

"Seems like every now and then, your brother just up and runs off into the woods and keeps going and going until he shoots off a bluff or falls into a gulley or under a logging truck or out of a tree, and then somebody's got to go look for him and haul his rear end battered and bloody out of the woods and back to civilization. Last time when I found him, he was near death. So now he's taken off into the woods again. What gets into that boy?"

Sandy shrugged. "He's no good at explaining himself. And there's stuff he can't remember."

"Actually it was my grandson, young Roy and me, who found him," said Pat. "And of course we weren't looking for Joseph at all. This was the day after the credit union was held up. Everyone was waiting for the RCMP to come up with something. Everybody had one description or another of the culprits and their getaway truck. Nobody knew if they'd headed up the coast or down the coast. But if they'd gone up—and up would be the way to go for back roads and bush to hide in—unless they met a boat at Egmont or somehow managed to sneak onto the Earls' Cove ferry, they had to still be up there somewhere.

"But the cops were coming up with nothing, so finally a bunch of us got together. We can find these guys, we said. We've got manpower the Mounties don't. And we sat down—this was at the firehall in Madeira Park—and mapped out every little road that heads off into the bush between here and the Skookumchuck, and there's lots of them. It was a dim and rainy morning when…"

"Look," Sandy took her third sip. "I know all that." She finally recognized that it was brandy she was drinking. "So maybe there isn't anything more."

"Yeah…" Sandy could see Pat fast-forwarding his brain. He wasn't used to editing his stories. For sure he was one of her favourite customers, but the old guy sure liked to talk.

"Roy has this Toyota with big wheels, nice high clearance, like it was built to tow tanks out of battlefields. The bridge over

Sakinaw Creek is a mossy, busted up old thing but Roy drove over it with complete…"

"So, he was close to Revenant Bay."

"Not in particular." Pat sighed. Many times in the past three years, he had dined out one way or another on his story of finding Joseph Windebank. Most of his listeners had heard it so many times that they simply ignored the more boring parts. Pat was not used to editing it. "We crossed the bridge and a little ways after, came to a three-way fork. Some forks were more plugged than others with blackberry and alder and young…

"But Joey was on the fork that went to the old gravel company dock…"

"Well that was it." Without asking, Pat topped up her brandy. "Roy wanted to stick to the plan and work through each fork systematically, but I saw fresh tire marks and I told him that, in my opinion, the road to Revenant Bay had recently sustained vehicular traffic. So we took off… a mile or so later we came over a hill and darn near ran over your brother at the bottom. Lying there with his head busted open, stinking of blood, shit and seawater. There was no way to get an ambulance in there so we bundled him into the back seat and brought him down here to the clinic." Pat shook his head. "A miracle he made it back. Roy drives like hell. He bounced us around like rats in a cocktail shaker."

Sandy tried to picture it. "So he'd walked from the bay…"

"By his wet clothes, he must have come from there. Walked a couple of miles, soaking wet with a bad head wound, before crumpling into a heap there on the road." Pat hefted the bottle of brandy. "Would you like another?"

To her surprise, Sandy saw that her glass was empty.

"So if I can get snoopy... why do you ask? Surely this is all old news to you."

"It's just that..." Sandy said, "... he was getting better, and then he stopped. It's almost as if he doesn't *want* to get any better. You know... to get normal again. So I guess I figure... that if I can find out what happened..."

"I'm glad Walter went and got him this time and not me." Pat shook his head. "I hate that back road stuff."

24. The live tanks

At the beginning of the season, the forklift brings plastic totes as big as hot tubs from where they have been stacked at the foot of the hill since last summer. The totes are the blue-green colour of swimming pools. We call them "the live tanks" once they are filled with seawater. Here the captured prawns are kept alive in their plastic cages, waiting to be sorted and fingerpacked and assigned to the freezers in their cardboard boxes.

On slow days I help clean the tanks and the hoses that connect them with the pumps and the compressors that keep the seawater cool and full of bubbles. We drain tanks and tip them and blast them with a pressure washer. Whenever I look up Jag is watching me as I do this.

"Am I doing everything okay?" I ask. But something in the parking lot catches his eye, he turns and he walks away.

25. The gypsies

As Sandy walked up the ramp to the government dock a gold Pontiac sedan, a white van and a Ford pickup rattled into the parking lot. All vintage late-20th century models, bottoms rusting out from years of toting leaky sacks of live shellfish. Laughing and trading insults, oyster farmers piled out of the three vehicles. They ranged in age from sixteen to about seventy.

Everybody knew Sandy and greeted her as they stomped down the ramp in their workboots, gumboots or running shoes. As each one approached, Sandy remembered the correct spelling of his first and last name and Skookum account balance when last she'd looked at it. Joe Hubbard—$536.71... Richard Dzerzinsky—$206.15... Emmett Olafson—$913.69... and *oh god Felix—*

"Uh Felix, have you seen Walter Conacher..." As she spoke, her head was spinning from the shock of the entry that had appeared in her head. *Erlmann, Felix*—$1458.98.

One way or another all of the other oyster farmers knew Joey.

"...watch out Walter don't charge ya a finders fee..."

"Bears woulda et him..."

"He's lucky Walter didn't throw him back."

Felix shrugged. "He's back up at the pub."

26. In the clear air

Now I'm back at the fish plant, I start to complain along with everyone else. How the sun burns our necks on the loading dock, how even in setting it blinds the hard-working evening shift sitting outside on their breaks. How cold the freezers are, specially the blast freezer when it starts up, its cold breath parches your lips and nose and sears like flame. How hard the prawns struggle, how they move and hop and flip and hustle, and scratch uselessly at the lids of their cardboard coffins, until we slide them onto the freezer racks and latch them shut behind the heavy steel door.

From the loading dock a ramp goes down to the floats and the pump house. It's easy to walk up when the tide is high, but at low tide you might as well push your pickup up Mount Daniel as push a dolly loaded with full cages up that ramp, with the prawns wondering what the hell is going on as the seawater drains away, panicking and rattling the cold armour of their bellies and jaws.

The deckhands and their skippers swing the cages off their boats, soaking the weathered timbers of the floats. We slide dollies under the stacks and climb back up the ramp, sometimes two men to a dolly. The prawns are scrabbling in the clear air until we roll them up the ramp and unload them into the tanks. The prawns grateful, as each cage fills with bubbling water. Thinking, because they are for the moment saved, that maybe this is a new adventure starting.

27. The pendant

Sandy blinked as her eyes adjusted to the light inside the Legion. Having escaped the oyster farmers, she had spent five minutes sitting in her car in the Legion parking lot to clear her head of their miasma of oysters, salt mud and overdue bills.

Finally (*minus* $1458.98!) she went inside.

Scanning the faces at every table but refusing to catch anyone's eye, she made her way through the main room and out to the smokers' tent on the back patio.

Walter was the last man sitting where two tables had been pushed together, chatting with the waitress who was wiping them down. He looked surprised, not in a specially good way, when Sandy sat down across from him and ordered a club soda.

"Come to ream me out," he said, "for firing your brother?"

"I don't know what you're talking about." She looked around the familiar patio: the faded metal tables, the frayed blue tarp of the smokers' tent. It had been a while.

"I didn't want to. But I had to get someone else. I've done prawns with no deckhand before and it's a pain. I'm getting too old and I've got nothing to prove."

Maybe this wouldn't be so bad, coming back here, she thought. So far nobody was whispering and pointing, her ears weren't burning, and she didn't mind listening to Walter's bullshit.

"Not that I expected miracles," he said, "but it was a chance to spend some time together and you know, I felt it was working.

I could tell he was relearning a few old skills, I felt he was getting better…"

"So did I," Sandy said. "But he jumped off your boat."

Walter shook his head. "We didn't pull up anything you wouldn't expect if you're going to haul a whale's skeleton up off the bottom—where it's been sitting for a year. Big mass of bones. Covered with weeds and muck, little bottom-feeders skittling off it as it broke the surface. The last couple months, Joey's got used to yarding octopuses and wolf eels out of prawn traps. It was really just more of the same."

"So why did he freak out and jump off?"

"Well, like I say, it wasn't anything horrible. Bones and muck and rot, except for stuff that's man-made—odd bit of rope, bottle caps… and there was this."

Walter put a hand inside his jacket and started groping for a pocket.

"Hmm… I was sure it was right there…"

He started going through his pants pockets and Sandy looked through the door, across the uncrowded lounge. Drinking Pat's brandy had made her thirsty. She saw Karen leave the bar and move towards them one table at a time, Sandy's club soda perched at the edge of a loaded tray.

Walter stood up. Under his jacket he wore a vest full of pockets. He kept talking, conscious of his absurdity, as if this was a comic routine he had performed many times.

"Once he pulled himself onto the rocks, Joey took off into the woods and that was the last we saw of him. We couldn't drop everything and go beating the bushes, not with two boats working that close… ah. Here." He tossed something onto the table in front of her.

She picked it up—and dropped it as if it was red hot. A polished wooden amulet on a loop of fine chain.

Karen came out onto the patio, sliding the glass door shut behind her.

"Thanks dear," Walter pulled out his wallet as Karen put their drinks on the table. "Let me buy you a drink, Sandy."

"If Walter's buying," she said to Karen, "I'd like a brandy as well." Sandy looked vaguely away at the treetops beyond the patio wall, not looking at the amulet as if it was some tourist trinket that didn't concern her one bit. Then she looked back at Walter.

"Would you mind if I take this?"

"Ah, well…" Walter obviously did mind.

"I could show it to Joey. Spring it on him gently. See what he has to say."

The amulet was an eagle's head, carved in a style she would call "Haida totem knockoff," from some soft wood like fir, stained and varnished with two tiny staring jade eyes. Gingerly she put her fingers on it, then closed them. Sandy had always thought the amulet was an ugly thing, but Arden had liked it:

—*It's my St. Christopher's medal.*

—*Arden, it's an eagle.*

—*That's right. Good luck for travelers.*

"Does it mean something that you know of?" asked Walter. "Not one bit."

Arden had hung it from the rear view mirror of her Toyota.

"God knows where he thought he was going," Walter was saying. "It's just a couple miles to the highway from there, but it's easy to get turned around in the woods. We spent the rest of the day getting the whale's bones secured on shore and then did some halfhearted beating through the bushes. Toward dark Felix put a storm lantern out on his porch and I tied up at his dock for the night.

"Anyway I really couldn't sleep for thinking that he might come banging down the dock at any time. So before daybreak I fired up the boat and eased my way down the channel going dead slow. When I got to Paradise Resort I turned around and came back, just as slow. I pulled into Revenant Bay to shut the engine off and maybe hike up that road a bit and call Joey's name and there was the strangest thing. A little doe came rustling out of the bush, took a look at me, and headed down the road. Then a minute later out comes Joey hobbling and blinking like a lost dog. He staggered out onto the float—he must have been pretty stiff sleeping out on the ground all night, and of course his feet were a mess. When he climbed out onto that old dock I thought he was going to take another header into the saltchuck. I had a hell of a time getting him into the boat."

"Do you think he found his way there on purpose?"

"On purpose?"

"Well, you know," she said. "It was the road to Revenant Bay where they found him after his accident."

"Never occurred to me," said Walter. "I assumed he just stumbled there. Think you might get anywhere by asking him?"

Sandy sighed. "Be my guest."

"Sorry to hear about Greg moving out."

"Thanks. It turns out we had irreconcilable differences. Differences that I was too dumb and insensitive to notice."

"But look at the upside," said Walter. "Here you are with me." He gestured around at the patio and the trees beyond, and raised his hand to catch Karen's eye as she made her rounds.

28. The borderland

I hear so many stories—in the lunchroom or at the Legion or on the road when I get a ride. Walter for example has fished up at the tops of the inlets, where the glaciers creep down to meet the ocean. Up there, he says, it is not like around here.

The inlets reach far into the mountains. It makes for a sort of borderland, Walter says, where different worlds meet. Sometimes they mix and sometimes not, like the two words he uses together. Rain shadow—on one side of the mountain, we get tree frogs and rain forest, but on the other side—this is what he tells me—sage brush and scorpions and rattlesnakes. Sometimes when a storm comes at us across the water, I can see the curtain of rain and I know that soon it will draw over us, and I think of those words, *rain shadow*, and when it passes over us, everything will have changed.

But I am always wrong. We zip our jackets, the storm passes over and nothing is changed except that the wind is up and there is a bit of chop.

What I am told is that some people will not go up those inlets. They refuse. They have heard the stories about wendigos and sasquatches and ghost bears, and other things that come out of the gorges at night, or slither up from the dark bottom of the saltchuck, their dorsal spines a white hiss along the black surface.

It is the borderland, so what is true one minute is sure to change, even more than you might normally expect. Deer that lead hunters far into the woods then vanish. Rogue bigfoot that heave rocks down at prospectors, but disappear before a rifle or a camera. Ghost houses rotting away in the trees, the people who built them never heard from again (there are lots of stories about the bush). They went into these forests to build new lives for themselves. They didn't come out.

I have heard that sometimes there are strange lights and sounds up on Mount Hallowell at night, but if you come close, the lights fly up into the sky. A fisherman told me that one sundown when he was crossing over the deepest part of Hotham Sound, a huge shape glided under his boat. He thought it was a whale, until it turned in the water and he saw its dead black eyes and its pale belly. "I swear it was a Great White," he told me, his eyes wide, "big as a bloody submarine!"

The bush is beautiful from a distance but it doesn't let you in easy, and sometimes if you get in, you want out ASAP. It is a place full of shadows, shadows that whisper there is no place for you here. No light comes from above, only from sideways, wherever you can find a break in the trees—that light through the trees, it is the ocean, and you must learn to walk toward that light, and walk fast, if you want to be saved.

I would rather look at a postcard of those hills—"Greetings From Beautiful Jervis Inlet, British Columbia"—than go into that borderland, and find what's in those trees. Sometimes you do not come out. I have heard about them finding boats that are just drifting, radio on, cups of coffee half-finished, nobody on board.

I hear so many stories, and it is hard for me to believe that people would keep telling them if they weren't true.

29. The herring mirror

After a while I got pulled off the fingerpacking and Rose got me back up to speed on some of the grading jobs that I had done before but now forgotten. This included mixing up "the chemical."

"The chemical" is delivered to us as boxes full of white powder sealed into one-kilogram bags. I empty a bag into a plastic tote out on the dock and, as the powder spills out, blast it with a freshwater hose. As the level rises, the powder and the churning water rise up together in a fine mist. I read the label on the plastic bag, pronouncing each word slowly to myself:

(FOOD ADDITIVES)

OXINON. W

ANTIOXIDANT AND GLAZING AGENT FOR RAW SHRIMP

INGREDIENTS

SODIUM METABISULFITE...17.5%

SODIUM ERYTHORBATE...10.0%

SODIUM POLYPHOSPHATE...7.5%

SODIUM ALGINATE...3.0%

DEXTRIN (MALT DEXTRIN)...62.0%

DIRECTIONS FOR USE:

(1) USE FOR EXPORT ONLY.

(2) SAFE QUANTITY OF OXINON.W

a. DISSOLVE OXINON.W IN 30 GRAMS (PER LITER OF WATER) IN WATER.

b. SOAK PRODUCT IN THE WATER SOLUTION FOR ONE MINUTE BEFORE FREEZING.

NET WEIGHT 1KG

We dissolve this stuff in water and douse the prawns in it so they will stay pink when they freeze and not turn gray. One night I asked Duncan why the mist stings my nose. Duncan was the only male on the crew who hadn't been fired the night I arrived. Duncan has been to sea, he can fix stuff. He is at age fifty even older than myself.

"Don't worry about it," he said. "It's the same shit they use in ice cream."

It was shaping up to be a busy night at the plant. Rolling the dolly to the edge of the loading dock I leaned over and saw colours down in the water—a mirror of light bending and flashing, like sunlight through leaves, and sending back a reflection, a picture of myself leaning over the dock. There was a tornado of fish down there, with little fish swimming up from the bottom of the twister, getting sucked up to the outer edges, or stuck in the middle chasing their tails in tight hard-working circles.

Why are they doing this, I thought. It is like a dance. They are not worried about a thing, not seemingly. They are happy as long as they whirl together down there doing, uh, whatever it is they're doing.

Duncan came up behind me, carrying a new fitting for the saltwater hose. I asked him what kind of fish those were and he said, "I thought you were fingerpacking today."

I stuttered, "I stayed to help the night crew. I'm doing the grading. They need prawns."

Duncan nodded his head at the water. "Those are one-year-old herring," he said. "It's good that they're doing that. There was a long time, you didn't see herring in the harbour like that." He took the fitting and headed down the ramp to the pump house. I looked over the rail. The wheel of herring had turned down deeper into the water, and my reflection was gone.

Rose had told me which live tank had the prawns we needed. But watching the herring had bumped out the memory of what I was doing and now I had to start over.

I pulled up the lid of live tank C1 and looked in. No prawns. Just cold seawater, a froth over its surface from the air bubbling up out of its tubes. I found prawns in C4 but I knew—because I had put them in there—that they were from the *Loafs & Fishes* that had just come in. We are supposed to process the prawns in the order that the boats bring them in. I needed prawns that had come in before the *Loafs & Fishes*. By the time I got to B2 Rose could see me from her office window. She put her hands together like a church steeple. I could see how she drew back the sides of her mouth and aimed the sound at me through her front teeth, A, and then bit down and blew as she held up four fingers. I grabbed a gaff hook, pushed the lid off of A4 and began yarding cages of prawns up out of the icy water.

30. Baby seals

We heard someone thumping up the stairs during the next break. I turned expecting to see Duncan but it was Jag, slamming a rolled-up *Province* into his hand.

"Lookit this." He slammed the paper down on the table where we were having coffee. I saw a headline *Saltspring Seal Pup...* and then Jag snatched it up and slid it down the table to someone else. "Might as well show it to someone who can read."

"Uh, actually…"

"*Saltspring Seal Pup Gets Second Chance,*" one of the guys read. A family on Saltspring Island found a baby seal on their beach. It was hurt so they bundled it up and took the ferry into Vancouver so they could take it to the Aquarium. At the Aquarium they would fix it up.

" 'So it can be restored to its natural habitat,'" he read out loud.

"So I can draw a bead on it!" Jag blurted out. "Saltwater cockroaches! I've pulled in so many salmon, still wiggling with one big bite out of them, nothing to do but toss 'em back. At least a killer whale takes the whole fish. Seal takes one bite and moves on.

"Don't look at me that way you fucking retard," he said to me. "Your buddy Walter Conacher has taken down more seals than salmon in his day."

I knew that Walter didn't like seals. That was one of the reasons he liked prawns: because we fish so deep, seals are not a factor. They don't raid the traps like they raid salmon fishermen, ripping into the nets to get at the squirming fish.

"Back in the glory days of gillnetting," Jag said, "Walter had a rack with his .30–30 on his cabin wall, and he had a handwritten sign under it that read, SEALS.

"Under the .30–30 was another rack with his .22, and under it was a sign that read, BABY SEALS." All the guys laughed—after a second, I laughed too.

31. The flames

With the job forcing me every day to leave the safety of the trailer I started thinking. At some point I would have to face up to Walter. He had been my friend and I had good and screwed him. Now when he brought his prawns to the plant he looked past me and, as there were always several of us helping, he would talk loudly and look into the distance, as if addressing not one of us but a crowd.

Sure you can handle all those? That ramp is soaking wet—don't go spilling my prawns back into the drink! Jeez, you boys need a hand? Only if someone he knew well came along, one of the other skippers or even Jag or especially Rose, would his voice drop and Walter sound like his old self.

Now if he drives by me on the way into Madeira, he never stops, even if he sees me picking my way along the shoulder in the rain. He no longer waves or honks, even if for a split second our eyes meet as he speeds past. By the time I raise my arm he is gone.

One Friday he didn't bring his prawns to the plant. "Engine trouble" we heard. We finished early that day—I helped the oyster farmers with their weekly shipment, then Rose told me to take off. "By the time these guys wrap it up," she said, "the evening shift will be here, give yourself a break."

I hitched a ride into Madeira Park and got dropped off at the Oak Tree, the old general store that guards the entrance to the mall. I could hear in the distance the buzz of a motor. The sound got louder as I crossed the mall parking lot and walked past the community centre. By the time I reached the ramp of the government dock I wondered if Walter had anything to do with this racket. I turned onto the commercial float where the fishermen tie up and as I got to his moorage I recognized the sound; it was a chainsaw. As I walked along the float I heard the saw gutter out and stop. There in the silence before me lay the *Medusa Deep*.

It looked as if it had taken a torpedo in the stern. Blue smoke billowed out of a huge hole in the rear deck, and all around the hole was fishing gear and engine parts. Someone was clunking around down there. Walter's old Stihl bobbed up out of the hole and his hand put it to rest on top of an upended plastic bucket, then disappeared down below.

Given our falling-out, I was afraid to step on board without an invite, but the chainsaw wobbling on top of the bucket started to worry me. If it fell onto the deck it would break something and if it fell back into the hole it would bust Walter on the head.

A tour boat left the marina next door and as soon as it cleared the dock the pilot stepped on the gas. The bow reared up, the tourists hung onto their Tilly hats, foam gushed out the stern and its wake slithered toward us like a serpent. As Walter's boat started to rock, I jumped on deck and grabbed the chainsaw. I heard a who's there and Walter's head popped up from the hole.

"I was afraid…" I waved the saw stupidly. "I saw this… I was afraid…"

"Put it down someplace where it *won't* bloody fall." Farther up the deck, out of the corner of my eye, I saw a flicker of blue flame. He steadied himself against the rocking of the boat. "Was that that asshole tour boat?"

"Yeah." I found a clear spot on the deck where I could put the saw.

"He pisses everybody off with his goddam wake. If you've come to ask for your old job back, forget it."

I looked around. The flame was gone.

"I want to apologize for jumping off."

"I hired one of the McMillan boys. He's dumb and unreliable but at least he doesn't jump on a chair when he sees a mouse."

"I don't know why I got so scared..." I choked up with guilt.

"I was having a hell of a time getting through this goddam season as it was. I took that day off as a favour to Felix. Then I had to keep fishing with no deckhand. Now I got a leaky gas tank." Walter shook a cigarette out of a pack, put it in his mouth. As the chainsaw exhaust cleared away I smelled raw fuel. "Felix thinks he'll mount those bones in a museum and make a million bucks."

Maybe even somehow the leaky gas tank was my fault. I wondered if there was any way that me jumping off the boat and swimming to shore had punched a hole in the *Medusa Deep's* gas tank. Maybe somehow, in that chain of circumstances...

With the ocean there is so much you don't see. It is a power huge and cold and mean that forgives nothing and nobody and it has a thousand faces. When we'd hauled up the bones the other fishermen had seen a huge soggy bundle with a little bunch of sticks and rubbish on top, but right away I had seen some sort of necklace and heard a voice, a woman sad and cold and unforgiving.

"You like it back at the plant?"

"Oh sure."

"Rose hire you back?"

"Rose hired me right off. Jag didn't act very happy, but now he seems okay. Now he's being really nice to me."

"Watch your ass if that bastard's being nice to you. Dammit!" Walter took the cigarette out of his mouth and looked at it, then put it back. "You. Rose." he said. "Together at the fish plant."

"Yup." I looked around. Maybe there was some tool or art object or conversation piece on the deck that I could talk about.

"Jesus I'd sure like a smoke about now." Walter looked down into the big pit he'd chopped in his boat. Bits of tobacco fell off his cigarette. "Forget it Joseph, I don't mean anything. You've caught me at my most pissed-off. Boat started to stink of fuel. Don't mention this at the plant, but your Japanese clientele might get a few funny-tasting prawns. I've got a new tank landing here, supposedly, in about fifteen minutes. Robbie went for coffee an hour ago and that's the last I saw of him."

The sun was getting low in the west. But the summer was coming. It would still be hours until full dark.

"I could use a hand," said Walter, "You just have to not mind screwing up your back for the rest of your life."

My mind raced for a clever reply. "That's okay."

Walter laughed. "I'm sure I'll someday discover Joey that you had a perfectly good reason for jumping ship that the rest of us just aren't in on."

He started handing up jerry cans of fuel and soon we cast off from the float. I took the end of a rope and walked along the gunwales of the other boats towards the dock. If anyone was on their boat I'd say excuse me and they would nod or say watch the bollard there, but there were not many people around. It was late in the day, the fishermen were out fishing or had gone home. I climbed onto the ramp and walked up to the dock with the end of the rope. Then I pulled the *Medusa Deep* into the dock until Walter could tie up to the pilings. We used the dock's crane to lift out the old gas tank ("I warn you it's a horrible sight," Walter said, "but please don't go leaping off the dock.") which indeed looked as if it had some horrible disease. Just as it touched the dock a truck pulled up and in an hour, with a lot of grunting and swearing, we had the new one lowered into the hold.

"Now all I've gotta do," Walter said, "is bolt it down and connect the lines and take her for a test run and then rebuild my deck. And then try, before the season ends, to catch enough prawns to pay for it all. If the competition hasn't scoured the ocean bottom clean."

Meanwhile he drove me down the road and bought me a beer at the Legion. His new deckhand Robbie was there already at a tableful of young guys. He made a great show of looking at the clock, and telling Walter he had lost track of the time.

"You better keep on your toes if you want to keep your job," Walter said. "If this seasoned professional hadn't happened by, I'd be cursing your name." He pointed at me, and for a second I got scared that he wanted me back fishing. Then he and Robbie started to discuss plans for tomorrow.

"I run a tight ship," Walter said and everyone laughed.

Why should I tell them, I thought, about the pendant hanging from the bones—that when I saw it, I saw flames rise from the deck and from the skeleton and even liquid fire gushing off the bones into the bay. That in diving into the water to save myself, I had saved all of them as well.

32. The hidden half of the world

Whenever Sandy broke any rules at work she did so noisily. Her theory was that if she let everyone in on it, nobody could blow the whistle on her afterwards.

For example, driving the forklift. "If they can't load 'er up quickly for you," she would say when closing a sale, "I'll jump on the forklift and do it myself." Indeed Greg, in his pre-Ginny period, had shown her how to run the forklift and she had nervously moved a skid of patio furniture. Lots of the workers there drove it, even though you were supposed to have the certificate. Sandy was, as far as she knew, the only woman. Although she considered it dead easy, she was an amateur and was terrified that somehow someday she would actually be called upon to use the forklift with customers watching.

So in other words, she thought as she spat in her mask and checked her regulator, she noisily announced she was breaking the rules only if she wasn't in fact going to do it. When she genuinely broke the rules like now, diving alone off a wrecked dock into Revenant's Bay, she kept it as secret as possible.

It had been a long time since she had dived but she hadn't forgotten the cardinal rule.

The forest came down to high tide line, and a little creek cut a slowly-deepening rut through the gravel into the saltchuck. Revenant Bay had once been one of the many charming little coves the coast had to offer. Twenty years ago a consortium from Vancouver had discovered a gravel deposit a few hundred yards in from the shore. They'd renamed the bay, built the dock; bulldozed a road in from the highway; cleared a staging area, and promptly gone bust.

Now the bush was reclaiming it. Branches whisked at her antenna and side mirrors; blackberries, ferns and alder shoots whacked at her Ford's underside and once there had been a deadfall: a windblown fir sapling just thick enough, she figured, to really bang up her little Escort if she tried to ram her way through. She almost turned back, but remembered that in the trunk along with the diving gear was Greg's old machete. She attacked the fallen fir and in a couple of minutes made a gap big enough to drive through.

Unless someone took some initiative, she thought, in a year or two—less if there's a serious winter storm—I won't be able to make it in at all.

But now she'd made it, the old Escort was cooling and ticking in the overgrown gravel clearing, the wind rippled the surface of the bay and she shivered.

Never dive alone.

After talking to Pat and then Walter, Sandy had developed a theory. The men in ski masks who robbed the credit union had driven off in a Dodge pickup and headed north up the coast, which didn't make much sense. Down the coast—south—was Vancouver and a thousand places to hide. Up
the coast was the ferry to Powell River and a handful of back roads to nowhere.

Whatever the plan had been, in Sandy's scenario they had decided to switch vehicles to cover their tracks, and Arden's was the unlucky vehicle they had picked. Beat the shit out of Joey—left him pretty near dead—and made off with Arden and her car. No one was looking for a terrified woman driving a beat-up little white Toyota with three nondescript male passengers. They could get on and off ferries with ease.

But the pickup had never been found. Just Joey—on the road to Revenant Bay.

The bay. Sandy bet there was something in the water there.

The gravel company's trucks had brought in tons of rip rap to build up the shore six feet above the high tide line. They had built a dock for small boats, but the barge dock had never materialized. Like the company's new name for the bay, everything was just too heavy and unwieldy. A plywood sign rotted in the weeds: *Titan-Colossus*.

In the early 1800s the crew of an English ship came ashore for water and afterwards complained about nightmares. The place went onto the charts as Revenant Bay and Revenant Bay it remained to this day.

Sandy told herself she was staying close to shore and diving no deeper than fifty feet. This was no guarantee of safety, but it was the best she could do. If she brought a partner she'd have to tell them what she was looking for. She'd feel like an idiot if she didn't find it and if she did find something, she wasn't sure she wanted anyone else to know.

She looked for the best place to dive. She would have preferred to wade in from the beach, but the wall of riprap was too steep. She didn't want to haul all her gear down there.

If you had your pickup right about where I'm parked, Sandy thought as she looked around the bay, you'd have a good hundred feet to fire it right off the edge of the rocks into the deep water.

The tide was coming in and the trips down to the dock with her gear were fairly easy. Back at the car she thought, now the hard part starts.

She looked out at the channel. There was a boat or two, far offshore. Probably nobody even noticed her car, a speck against the tree line. Still, she opened the passenger door for cover and hurriedly stripped off her clothes and into her bathing suit. She hadn't worn it since last summer and thought hey, it goes on pretty easy. *As long as I don't try to snack away my aggravation, depression and abandonment I'll be fine.* It was the wetsuit that showed the awful truth. She hadn't used it in a few years and it had clearly shrunk. Getting one leg on was a struggle. She managed to work it over both feet and then put on her shoes so she could jump on the rocky ground, feeling the blood forced into her torso as the suit was forced reluctantly up her legs. By the time she zipped up the front she felt like she had a python wrapped around her.

Breathless and sweaty, down on the float she grabbed her dive flag and with fifty feet of line, threw the anchor off the end of the dock out as far as she could. As the line sliced through the water, she picked up the flag itself and tossed it away from the dock, so it wouldn't get snagged. The flag bobbed on its little float and then disappeared, snatched under the surface.

Deeper than I thought. Sandy hefted her weight belt and secured it around her waist and sat down on the edge of the dock, put on her fins, wrangled herself into her tank and hooked it up to her buoyancy compensator. She spat in her mask and put it on, got the regulator in her mouth and took a couple of deep breaths. The python was not only squeezing her, it was a big one, and she was carrying its full weight. No longer suited to this world, if she stayed up here in the air she would surely die.

Sandy pushed herself into the water. She flinched at the change of element and temperature, the irrational moment of passing from open air to underwater. Then all her troubles fell away. She was free with a whole ocean before her. The hidden half of the world.

33. New words

I learned words like *fathom, double haul, berried females, scotchman* and *deep line* on Walter's boat.

At the plant, hanging out with the guys on the evening shift I learn words like DUI, *possession, drunk and disorderly* and *uttering threats.*

"Zero," one of them says one night. "How 'bout a brand new IBM Thinkpad? Plays DVDs. Lotsa RAM. You can play games. Three hundred bucks."

I'm thinking. "Can I go on the internet with it?"

"I wouldn't do that. But it's a great machine."

"Zero, you can live without it," Duncan says.

It's Blair who's selling the Thinkpad. Big young guy, tall and fat, shaven head. Blair lives with his mother and his teenage girlfriend down in Sechelt.

"Jeez thanks man," he says bitterly. "I'm trying to make a buck here."

Duncan says to me, "There's a reason you can't go online with it."

He tells Blair, "If someone IDs it online and chases down Zero, you know he'll tell him where he got it. Then whose ass gets fried?"

I can't answer that question. Playing DVDs sounds pretty cool. But my hospital therapist, Amber, had spent a lot of time drilling me about not spending money. The rule was, Stop and Think. *Stop and Think.*

So I stop and think. While I'm thinking, the skipper of the *Hands Up* stops in for coffee and Blair sells him the laptop.

34. Freezer burn

Walter (now that I'm forgiven), that angry woman who comes to my trailer, Rose at the plant—my past is explained to me, over and over yet it remains a half-drawn map. Place names, but no connecting roads or shorelines. No clue of how I might get there from here.

To other people, their lives make perfect sense. But I feel like I've been pushed onstage and just before me, in the dark theatre, there is an unseen audience, each of them holding the script that I am missing.

The memories of what I have tasted and touched and seen for myself don't amount to much. For everything else, I can only believe whatever I see and hear, and try to link that up with such little bits as I remember. There are popups, pictures that suddenly appear and bob around from one side of my vision to another and are then gone. Still, I got some strange notions the last time I loaded a reefer truck.

Every week or so a refrigerated truck takes away a full load of prawns. That is one of the hardest days. A truckful of frozen prawns is worth a lot of money. The owners are here from Vancouver. Rose acts different—not only because of the tight schedule but because she has to show the owners that she's a take-charge kind of plant manager. We fill up the skids as fast as we can, but we are supposed to work not only at lightning speed, but with a light touch.

"Go easy on those boxes!" Rose barks. As we stand in the freezer nervous at being yelled at, waiting for the forklift to take out the full skids so we can throw down empty ones and fill them up, Derek, a young blonde guy who hates to be yelled at, assaults one of the cardboard boxes and sinks his teeth into it, making little growling sounds. We laugh. In a couple of months in Japan, some grunt like us will be wondering about those tooth marks.

Then again we go go go, hand-bombing the boxes onto skids and chasing the forklift like hockey players worrying a puck as the load bounces out to the truck, and then off the skids into the truck. We have to do it all in the hour and a quarter between the time the truck backs up to the plant and the time it has to leave to catch the next ferry to Horseshoe Bay. Miss that deadline and the truck has to sit around two more hours, all systems roaring to keep the product cold, its driver getting overtime, the warehouse in Richmond staying open late… it costs everyone, the bosses remind us, shaking their heads as if, because of our neglect and no conscience, the worst has already happened.

Rose flutters around, checking that we put the right boxes on the right skids—one skid is all medium, one skid is all large—and a guy from head office is there to crack the whip. As soon as one of us gets off the forklift, he is eager to jump into the driver's seat and show us how they do it in town. We pack the boxes of frozen prawns into the truck, leaving just enough space inside each layer to circulate the cold air. Finally, we pack the truck so tight that we throw ourselves against the door to force it shut.

At the end, the truck with its tons of prawns grinds up the hill, bounces onto the road and heads for the ferry. Rose turns off the storage freezer and I defrost it. With a crowbar I break up the hardest lumps and shovel the busted ice through the ribbon door onto the loading dock.

By then, my back aches and sometimes I get the freezer burn. You need to put on the right gloves, but you are always taking them off and putting them on when a truck is in. Sometimes you don't have them in the right place at the right time, there is a lot to do and everyone is all in such a big hurry.

Freezer burn—as if pushed to their farthest ends, cold and heat turn into the same thing.

The day after I helped Walter with his boat was a truck day. I got to work early, we loaded the truck in time, at the end there was slush and shattered ice all over the plant floor… "don't worry about that," Rose said, "it'll be gone by the time the night shift gets here." Then she hurried off… a boat had radioed that it was on the way in and now she could see it foaming towards us from the mouth of the harbour.

Afterwards I went home to the trailer and took off my new gumboots. I thought of oyster seed fluttering through cold water, somewhere on the bottom of the bay at Felix's where I jumped off. It swims onto one of my old boots that lie there in the muck. The seed is too tiny to see, soft as butterfly dust and it touches the slimy gumboot with a shy little foot. This is good, it thinks; and the seed glues itself on the black surface. Soon white dots of oysters are budding all over. Prawns sniff the rich smells of the dark opening and skitter away—something big has taken over the boot, there is a crab or wolf eel or octopus living there, but all over the boot, mussels and oysters are cemented into place and they feel safe there.

I pour some water into my tea kettle and stand at the stove to make sure I turn it off when it starts to whistle. Into a cup of steaming water I dump a spoonful of instant coffee. The crystals disappear under the water, then rise again to burst over the surface like an octopus spreading out its long tentacles to reveal its true size. It blossoms like a flower under the water.

I sit on the front step. If I sit there long enough, I will get hungry and get up and get something to eat, and so I sit there and wait for that time. I hold up my hands in front of me. They are big hands and the fingertips are red. Freezer burn. I look at my hands and I have an odd thought. I think, *there is something that must be true, and it is not this.*

35. The charm

Something flashed in the dark water below. It was the dive flag. She'd given it fifty feet of line, and it was already that far down. Sandy cleared her ears as she pulled herself down the line. Off to the side, there was something that looked out of place.

Underwater, the Revenant shoreline sloped into the rich green water of Agamemnon Channel and plummeted into blackness at the mouth of the bay. Here and there great ruts had been carved through the silt and gravel where boulders, used to fill in the foreshore, had escaped the riprap and tumbled into the dark.

Sandy was on the lookout for something the size and shape of a Dodge pickup with crewcab. Popular accounts had it as gray with a red stripe along the side, although after three years she expected it to be covered with mussels and barnacles. And God knows what else. There was stiff competition for territory in these fertile waters. New surfaces didn't remain untenanted for very long.

But what she found was not a truck at all.

The slope was gentler here, and rather than continuing its plunge down the bank of the channel, a boulder as big as a washing machine had come to rest against an outcropping of rock, and later something else had come to rest against the boulder.

Covered with algae, barnacles and patches of rust was a two-door white Toyota, lying upside down with the driver's side crammed against the rock. The front end was crumpled and both doors were open. Sandy pulled a flashlight off her belt. A shred of fabric waved from the handle of the open door.

Sandy paused before the door. She'd ridden in this car more than once. She pushed herself towards it until her gear clanked against the passenger door and shone the light inside. Among the debris on the flipped-over ceiling she spotted the rear view mirror, and when she reached down and grabbed it, the
mirror came off in her hand. Missing from it was Arden's familiar jade-eyed charm—good luck for travelers. Of course it was missing, it was a hundred yards away, safely in Sandy's purse, locked into the trunk of her Escort.

Amid the muck on the ceiling she saw a canvas deck shoe, a crab scuttling away from her light.

The bubbles from her respirator darted up past the dangling seat belts and were caught in the seats, creeping across floating bits of debris. The only floating thing still intact was a styrofoam coffee cup. Disturbed by her entry, the bubbles gathered and broke apart and slid this way and that, hoping to find a way out of the car and up to the surface. Sandy shone her light there and under the passenger seat. A wolf eel glared back at the flashlight beam, ghoulish, nervous and ready to defend this rare and special territory.

That was it. There was nothing else in there. Sandy started to back away but the door thumped against her and something pulled. She felt panic clawing at her. She tried to ease to the side to free herself. She pushed forward; then she tried to back up but got hooked again. Movement caught her eye. It was just her own bubbles, coming more rapidly now.

She had a half hour of air in her tank. She reached down to her waist—where was the knife? She pictured it still locked into the trunk of the Escort along with her purse and Arden's good luck charm. Then she pictured it in a cardboard box at the police station in Sechelt with the rest of her personal effects, handed over to a stunned and grieving Greg, eyes welling with remorse.

Reaching up and back in her tight wetsuit, she checked her tank hoses—all clear at the top but the BC hose was stuck on the door handle. It was a moment's work to wiggle it off, back up and she was free.

Real smart, *Alexandra.* She was more scared than she thought she'd be. So far the worst hadn't happened, but she'd sure set herself up for it. *Never dive alone.* She looked up at the dive flag. It moved, beckoned to her to follow the currents that urged everything in their embrace deeper into the channel. She wondered how long the water had taken to sweep up Arden, how far it had taken her out into the channel. She swam to the flag, pulled its anchor up off the bottom and swam hard to pull it into the shallow water so the flag would break the surface. Once she was up there, safe again in her real element, she could haul it in.

36. The live truck

I ask Rose if I can drive the live truck sometime.

"Joey, I don't think so."

"I used to drive all the time," I say. "I'm pretty sure."

"That was before," Rose says. "You know, you need to have a driver's licence. You need to have it on you when you're driving. Let's see your licence."

I put my hand on my new wallet, which is in my jeans under my smock. Not much in there. I try to think of some smart remark.

"Well," I say. "If that's... if that's..."

Rose is jealous, I decide. She thinks I want to get close to Barb.

Barb is a big fat pretty woman, and she jokes with me—hey there cutie she says—almost to the point where I joke back. She has long dark hair and there are two girls, her daughters, who come to the plant and fingerpack every season.

It is really Barb's job I want. She drives the live truck. Of all the jobs at the plant, this one is the greatest. She drives up and down the coast from dock to dock, hanging out with the skippers, selling them bait and loading up their prawns. I bet I could do that job. I would work fast, especially when the days were hot. Slide the plastic cages straight off the boat into the back of the live truck where the prawns could take deep breaths of cold salt water and chitter back and forth, shaking their bony tails.

"Joey, you're doing fine here at the plant," Rose said, "and Barb is doing fine driving the live truck. If she ever can't make it, there's Duncan and Jag and even me, we all can drive it just fine."

We were in the office upstairs at the plant. I bit my lip and started to head towards the door. Just then Barb appeared in the door, panting a bit from walking up the long flight of stairs.

"Hey Barb," I said. "Do you think I can drive the live truck sometime... you know, if you can't make it?"

"You'll hafta ask Rose," she said. I snorted in frustration and walked past her and clomped down the stairs.

37. The dinosaur birds

On the way out this morning I fussed with locking the trailer door. The door doesn't close well—the latch has been bent somehow. I tried and tried to get it locked and then gave up. I threw my backpack over my shoulder and looked up at the cliffs that overlook my trailer and Rondeview Road and the trees in the hollow behind it that slopes down to a nameless pond. I heard cries from the sky over the cliffs. Two blue herons circling in a way that herons do not usually do.

On the other side, the cliffs look out over Malaspina Strait and on this side they look down at me. The trees on this side of the cliffs are fine, but the trees facing the ocean are bent and stunted. When it storms their roots tug and stretch and break away from the coastal rock. When it's hot they clench all the harder into the cliffs, sucking every bit of water out of every crack and shred of soil. It is a hard life, on the ocean side of the cliffs. Down where I was, I could not see out to the strait, but the herons were warning me. They were horking and cackling about something they could see out there. Their voices are like rocks grinding together, and they are big creatures. Watching them fly in circles, listening to their creaks and groans echo off the cliffs—nothing else sounds like that—it was as if they were dinosaur birds. From the ocean there had blown a wave of time, and when the wave had washed over them, suddenly it was a million years ago, and until the wave passed they would not be the same and they were warning me.

A wave is sweeping in from the sea they warned. Zero, the cliffs cannot stop it.

I pictured it in my head. A wave of time, and in the wave was music, and faces I didn't know, the roar of something old and big and hungry. You don't need these people, the voice said. I don't need this I replied, I don't need to go back nor forward. A dinosaur's hot breath just over my head. Down under the water I thought, it's safe and cool, and time does not pass down there. I started back inside my trailer.

If I stay in the trailer, I thought, the wave of time will wash right past me. Someone else can worry about time—let someone else have it. I shut the door. Up on the cliffs, I could hear the birds calling in their angry voices. There was a *Harbour Spiel* on the table and I took a pencil and wrote a word on the border of the cover.

Lookit that—spelled perfectly, I thought. I ripped the border of the magazine and looked around for a place to dump it. All I want is to go down to the plant and go on pogey this winter. I want Rose to call me again in the spring.

But if I stay in the trailer, I thought, if I was late for the plant or didn't show up at all, it would be a mark against me and Rose wouldn't be calling me in the spring. I could chance anything but that.

I tried again, inching out onto the porch. On the horizon the birds were gone. I stumbled out to the road and started jogging to make up for lost time. Still running, I looked at the word on the scrap of paper. *Pterodactyl.* I stuck it in my mouth and chewed up the bit of paper with the word on it. Looking back over my shoulder as I ran, I chewed it into pulp and spat it into the blackberries.

38. The Mount Hallowell vampire woman

"He's on a toot."

"…finally got laid, doesn't want to come back to work and break the spell."

"…found something better than this bullshit…"

Brandon, one of the young guys on the night crew, hadn't come to work for two days. Hadn't called in. No one could raise him at home.

I came to the Legion with Walter, we took a table and soon there was a circle of chairs around us—some of the young guys from the plant, the bagpipers after their weekly rehearsal, some prawn fishermen who, like Walter, after six weeks of eighteen-hour days seven days a week, figured they needed a night out.

"…car broke down…"

"…hasn't paid the phone bill…"

Although we started off all worried about Brandon, conversation soon drifted to what a loser he was and how dead certain it was that whatever happened to him was his own damn fault… Next it drifted back again to his many fine qualities and how life can be a big ripoff even for the best and smartest of us… then back to how sometimes, guys his age just got fed up and headed off to Vancouver to seek their fortune, and were such fuckheads and losers that they never told anyone…

"What none of you has brought up…" Walter began.

...or to another place just the other side of Vancouver—Alberta, which was a sort of oil-and-mud-filled version of the Prairies—and it would be a while before they were seen or heard from again...

"I maintain that anything can happen..." Walter said.

...or he might have got a deckhanding job and be fishing halibut off the Alaska panhandle where radio reception was lousy and cellphones didn't work...

"...especially in this place..."

...or he might have fallen off a boat and drowned, although in fact this hardly ever happens except at night to people that are pissed.

"For example," said Walter. "Nobody has brought up the subject of the Mount Hallowell vampire woman."

There was a moment's silence and then someone said, "Come off it."

"Isn't that her playing pool?" someone joked.

I looked over at the pool table. A blonde girl in tight blue jeans was leaning over to take her shot. Some of the guys had been shooting her glances and muttering jokes.

Without looking, "No resemblance," Walter said. "I don't even have to bring this up..."

Now the guys at the table started changing their tune. Come on Walter.

"No," said Walter, "you'll think I've gone soft in the head."

"Come on Walter," I said. "At least, I want to hear this."

"Okay Joey. But for the rest of you guys take this as a warning about your damn doubts and sarcasm because I wouldn't believe it either. Except, except—" Walter looked around the circle of faces, fixing everyone in the eye "—that it really happened."

"A year ago last fall I drove up the highway and back behind the hydro substation, up into the hills as far as I could go. I was supposedly out for deer. Anyway, I had my .30–30 with me, though to tell the truth I'm not much for hunting. My heart just isn't in it anymore. But Judy was on my case about a dozen different things. Nothing special—money, drinking, women, household repairs, the usual stuff—but it was a good excuse to get out of the house."

"I'd issue ya a license fer elk," said George, one of the pipers. The pipers all play golf and hate elk. They are always grumbling about elk shitting all over the greens and tearing them up.

"I drove up the side of Mount Hallowell until I came to the big earthwork that blocks the road. It's something only a serious four-by-four could get over. If I tried it in my F-150 I would just get hung up. Beyond that dirt barrier, the road switchbacks up the mountain to the old copper mine, and I'm told keeps going right to the top of the Caren Range. Be that as it may, it was the end of the road for me.

"It was getting late in the day. I had a few supplies and I decided to camp out. Maybe at the crack of dawn I'd take a look-round with the .30–30, see if I could get inspired to actually shoot at something.

"Then I got a fire going to heat up soup. I went to work with the axe and gathered up a decent pile of firewood. Night was setting in. Sleeping in the back of the truck amid the silence of nature started to look…"

"Janice," George called out to the bar. "Janice dear, could we get another round here?"

Walter stopped talking and glared at George.

"Walter's gettin' overly poetic…"

"This is a true story," said Walter, "but I'm trying to give it some background so you'll know exactly what went down."

"I thought I was gonna hear a ghost story, not goddam *Survivorman*."

"Be patient for chrissake." Walter took a deep breath.

"Of course once you get up in those hills you're in ten-year-old clearcut. The alders and the fir seedlings are twelve-fifteen feet high. There's lots of dry wood around to build a campfire, and the spot I'd found had a good view out over the strait. As the sun went down I could see clear over to Vancouver Island.

"It was the tail end of Indian summer. The autumn storms hadn't started, but the nights were getting chilly and I was getting ready to turn in.

"Then I heard something *howling* up on the mountain. First one animal, then another one joined it, then another. There haven't been wolves on this part of the Coast for a hundred years, so I figured it must be coyotes.

"Everything went dead quiet. The crickets and the tree frogs shut up. The wind stopped whispering through the firs. I couldn't even hear a boat engine out on the harbour. Night had come down, like a doubleglaze window, between the rest of the world and me.

"From farther up the road I heard what sounded like the chuffing of some big animal. I felt some concern. I went around to the cab and pulled the rifle out of its scabbard behind the seat. And loaded it.

"I looked up and saw someone standing on the earthwork barrier, looking down at me. They picked their way down it slowly, not in any hurry. I sat and watched them come. When the person got closer I saw it was a woman. She came out of the darkness and stood there looking at me. Just at the edge of the firelight, like she'd melt if she came any closer.

"'You hear that?' I said. 'It sounds like we've got wolves back on the coast.'

"She snickered. 'They're just dogs.'

"I cleared a place and finally got her to sit, but it wasn't easy. In fact I had a hell of a time coaxing her into the firelight.

"She sat there looking out over the fire into the darkness. I offered her some cheese and crackers. I offered her a taste of scotch. She said no to everything. Finally I got her to sit down at the other end of the tailgate from me.

"We sat there and I threw another stick on the fire. I tried not to stare but in the firelight I couldn't tell how old she was. Jet black hair. A nice-looking full-figured type, a bit on the short side.

"At first I figured she was a young girl up from town—I'd never seen her around before—and that the boyfriend would appear soon, we'd start up a big racket of goodwill and there'd go the rest of my crackers and scotch. Or that just up that mountain road, there was a father just about to show up to chaperone his little girl. Because every time I looked up she looked different. Hopping onto the tailgate she looked about sixteen, then gazing over the fire she looked more my age, maybe tinting her hair black and boasting a few grandkids. When she came out of the dark I figured her for an Indian—I mean a Native person—then when she sat down she looked like an English girl, then dark-haired and pale like a prairie Ukrainian.

"It got late and I'd had a few more scotches and I didn't see the point of building the fire up again. Can I give you a ride home or somewhere? I offered. No, she didn't need a ride.

"'Don't tell me you live up here,' I said. She just looked at me.

"'Actually,' she said, 'I was hoping I could stay here with you.'

"I climbed in the back of the truck to unroll my sleeping bag. While she was getting in under the canopy I started to undo my bootlaces, but in a second she was all over me. I never experienced anything like it."

Walter paused and no one else spoke up. I think everyone was wanting more details and expecting them. But all that Walter said was, "It seems to me… I think I had a good time… but you know what I remember most?"

"Sand in yer sleeping bag."

"Your first sex since the Canucks won the cup."

Walter leaned forward and his voice dropped almost to a whisper. "Her lips," he said, "and her tongue. They were goddam… cold." He shivered.

"It wasn't what I'd call a joyous union. It wasn't even one of those situations where you realize too late that the two of you are incompatible, but you can't agree to stop. If anything, it was like being raped by a good-size halibut.

"She was a hungry girl, she was all over me, and that's the last I remember. Honest to God, talk about falling under a spell. The next thing I knew I was nowhere near Mount Hallowell. I woke up on a stranger's lawn. I was in Garden Bay, down where the streets all have Indian names. It was cold, I was lying there in the dew, the sun was just up and my truck was in the ditch.

"I managed to rock it out of the ditch, drove home and took to my bed for two days. Judy thought I'd been out on a toot and had no pity for me. I never told her I was an innocent victim of the Mount Hallowell vampire woman."

"Jesus Walter," I said. "Jesus."

"Maybe she didn't like how you tasted," somebody said, "and threw ya back."

"I don't recall any complaints." Walter reached into his shirt and pulled out something on a chain. "Now Judy thinks I got religious because I've worn this ever since."

There was a little gold cross on the end of the chain.

"So you're saying that Brandon ran into this lady."

"I've got no evidence," Walter said, "one way or the other."

"D'ya think this creature's still up there?"

"With all do respect Mr. Conacher I don't believe a fuckin' word."

"Did ya get her phone number," said one of the younger prawn fishermen.

"Go ahead and be skeptical." Walter shook his head. "There are more things in heaven and earth than are dreamed up in our philosophies. What about you Joey? You have a contemplative look."

I was rolling my tongue against the inside of my mouth. "I can't tell if my tongue is warm or not." I licked my thumb. "I guess it is."

"It's what yer mouth is for," said George. "To keep yer tongue warm."

"Good excuse to keep your mouth shut," said Walter.

I said, "But I don't think I've ever felt anyone else's tongue."

The door buzzer went off and we all looked up. Janice went behind the bar to let in the newcomer. We watched the door open and there was Brandon.

39. The day the aliens landed

What had she expected? —A summer intern from Vancouver seated Sandy at the far end of a long table in the lunchroom of the *Raincoast Courier* in Gibsons. She put a cardboard box in front of Sandy and went away. At the other end of the table, three staff members, all women younger than her, glanced up and went back to critiquing images on a laptop. Over their shoulders Sandy could just see the screen.

The box held the *Courier's* back issues from two years ago. Sandy was looking for an issue in which, for once, Pender Harbour had made the front page.

"She *is* a doll," said one of the women. "You can't really blame him."
"Duhh! She's fifteen."
"The piece is supposed to be about D-Day veterans."
Sandy leafed idly through front pages, until there it was.

PENDER HOLDUP SHOCKS COAST

Pender Harbour residents' concern about the lack of police presence in their community was given a big boost by a mid-day robbery last Thursday.

Students were back inside the neighbouring elementary school after lunch hour when a pickup truck pulled into the handicapped space in front of the credit union next to the supermarket.

"It was a normal day," said a teller. "Then suddenly these three guys were here shouting and waving guns. It was like aliens had landed."

Wearing black ski masks and camouflage gear, the rifle-wielding robbers demanded entry to the credit union's vault and stuffed cash from the tellers into nylon overnight bags. One of them, for no apparent reason, even fired a shot into the ceiling.

"That's what really terrified everyone," said Diane Stall, assistant loans manager. "Up to that point we'd been going along with them, just like we'd been trained to do. But that gunshot was so loud in here and there was really no reason for it."

Sandy went to photocopy the clipping. The young women at the end of the table were looking at more pictures. Sandy recognized the annual sandcastle contest at Davis Bay. A clutch of young castle-builders, grimed with wet sand, waved their hands at the camera.

"I haven't looked like that in a bikini for a long time."

"Like you ever did!"

Putting a few coins in the jar next to the machine, Sandy made her photocopies and went back to her end of the table to search for follow-up articles. The thieves had jumped in the truck and taken off—according to some witnesses (*it had all happened so fast*) not south toward Sechelt, Gibsons and the Vancouver ferry but north, where there was nothing but back roads, the village of Egmont and the ferry to Powell River. Police had arrived a half-hour after the robbery, spent the next day searching and found nothing. The day after that, two members of a "community group"—that would be Pat and his grandson Roy—had found Joseph Windebank, shivering and half-dead from a head injury. But no one had ever found the money or the thieves or the pickup.

She was trying to piece the parts together. Arden and Joey up on that back road, possibly picking some of Arden's herbs or mushrooms. Or maybe, Sandy thought, they even had a secret little marijuana patch back there. The thieves pull in, demand their car at gunpoint. Joey gives them a hard time and gets beaten within an inch of his life. And then…

The wreck in Revenant Bay screwed Sandy's theory right up. Obviously these three brutes didn't jam their guns and their loot into Arden's Toyota and force her to drive them onto the Earls Cove ferry. While cops up and down the coast looked for their getaway pickup, they could have escaped up to Powell River and over to Vancouver Island.

But once they made their escape, Arden should have turned up somewhere dead or alive—the fatal flaw in Sandy's theory.

But then what happened, then what? Where did she go?

"Now this is too much," came a voice from down at the end of the table. "This is a chicken farm."

"Chicken?" Laughter, glances down the table at Sandy.

"He finds them everywhere!"

"You know," one of them said soberly, "I'm not sure it's hurting our business. The numbers keep creeping up."

Sandy put everything back where she found it and left with her copies, offering the photo-women a big smile as she squeezed past. *What if Joseph had been one of the masked men?* He was a try-anything kind of guy, and a good candidate for a get-rich-quick scheme. He and Arden never had a dime.

The car in the bay. Arden's car. What if she told anyone about it? If the police returned to the investigation, what would they find out? What would happen to her brother?

40. The women in the woods

Walter's story about the vampire woman changed everything. Would I have jumped ship and run into the woods if I'd known about her?

The story answered a lot of questions, especially about that feeling of being watched that I sometimes get in the woods. Who was it who spoke to me in a dream, and as the light came, who led me through the trees to the ghost clearing? Did they know what I was running from? Did they know that when I saw the wooden pendant on the body of the whale, and the flames rise from the deck, that I saw a woman's face in those flames.

For a while since Walter told his story, I stopped walking in the bush late in the day when the dark is coming. And I never walk on those slopes where a cliff has tumbled down into a skirt of rocks and rubble—that's where the salal grows. When you walk through those clusters of waxy leaves, you have to be careful where you step. With those gaps and cracks between the rocks, you could twist an ankle or break a leg or if the hole is big, who knows, even fall down among those cold rustling bodies that wait there in the dark.

It makes sense to me that this is where the vampire women live, driven by the dawn to slide back into the safe caves under the rocks. They lie there in peace—no one smart hikes across that treacherous landscape.

I got nervous about walking to and from Madeira Park at night, but then I thought, forget it. Walter invited that woman to sit with him, and then join him in the back of his truck. He met her halfway, at least halfway. I just don't think I'd be that stupid. A polite how dee do and keep walking. Don't even look her in the eye.

But it explains a lot about this thing: death. Does it happen right away or is it gradual. Do you sicken a bit at a time, rallying only to wander at night, into such deep woods that you want to wander there forever, until the need for warmth and well-lit places gets too intense. Or flip your back on the world of air and push away from the rocks, where a few feet from shore the bottom drops off into darkness.

I don't know if we would want to do that. Men are better off not being vampires, but if you are a woman you could do worse. I have been hearing talk that Rose is going to leave the plant before the season ends. This scares me. It must only be a stupid rumour. I can't imagine what she is going to do or why she is doing this.

What scares me about the vampire women is not that they suck blood or do whatever it is they do. It is that they want to live out there in the night, and I know how lonely it is out there.

41. The Canada Food Guide

I was watching an ad for an exercise machine. Thinking that like the ad said, it would make me look better and feel great about myself. I would have enhanced self-esteem.

I stood up and looked down at my body. I was wearing a tee shirt and jeans. There was a knock at the door, and Rose came swooping in.

"Joey," she said, "I've been thinking. We've got to do something about your lunches." She plopped a full shopping bag onto a chair, then cleared a space on the kitchen counter and looked for a cloth to wipe it. "And while we're at it, about your housekeeping."

"I like it here."

"Paradise for you. Hell for everyone else." Rose wetted some paper towels and wiped the counter. Then she took stuff out of the shopping bag.

"I've been noticing what you bring for lunch. Peanut butter and jam, some cookies, a can of pop. You're going to die of diabetes."

"I bring two peanut butter sandwiches."

"What do you eat when you get home?"

I didn't say anything. I wasn't sure it was any of Rose's damn business. She went over to the fridge.

"Milk good," she said, as if she was reading a checklist inside the fridge door. Pudding cups okay. Half a Sara Lee cheesecake okay." She rummaged around. "Where are your vegetables?" She gave up and came over to my chair. "What do you do for protein?"

I sighed and got up. I picked the Canada Food Guide off the fridge. The word protein rang a bell. I looked for it on the guide. "Protein, protein..."

"Meat," Rose suggested.

"I have hamburgers in the freezer." I opened the fridge. "Look: eggs." I double checked the Canada Food Guide.

"Look what I've got here," Rose said. She was buttering something. "Two slices of whole wheat bread."

"Yuck."

"You get to like it. Wash some lettuce leaves like this—where's a dish towel?"

"Lettuce... brown bread... fucking rabbit food."

"Don't you use that language with me and don't call it rabbit food. You sound like those young bozos at the plant—know nothing, do nothing, go nowhere."

I watched Rose slice some cheese. "Pepsi and potato chips," she continued. "Pop, greasy chips and those big chocolate cakes Barb brings up from Sechelt—no wonder they got shit for brains." She put the cheese on the bread and covered it with lettuce. "Would you like some onion on this, Joey?"

"Those big chocolate cakes? I love them."

Back in my fridge again, she opened the mayonnaise, made a face, screwed the lid shut and threw it in the garbage. "Joey, you've got a way to go. But look here." She put the sandwich together. "You've got a cheese sandwich in your lunch tomorrow. With lettuce."

"I like peanut butter."

"You're a big boy, we'll give you a peanut butter sandwich too." Rose made me one with brown bread.

Finally she said, "Look at this: you've got a cheese sandwich with lettuce, a peanut butter sandwich with jam, a banana and a can of juice." Rose wrapped the sandwiches in plastic and put everything in a bag in the fridge. "Now don't you forget that in the morning or you'll hurt my feelings." She made herself busy finding a bowl in my cupboards, then left it out on the counter with some bananas and apples in it.

Somehow the whole thing pissed me off. But I said, "Uh Rose, this is great."

"I'm leaving this stuff here. I want you to make a habit of this." Rose plopped a kitchen chair down next to my armchair. "What's on the tube?"

I wanted to sit down too, but somehow I couldn't, not with Rose there. "It's about exercising."

"We get enough darn exercise when the season's on." Rose found my remote and started clicking though the channels on the TV. "On my time off I sleep like…"

"Watching that show, I was wondering if I was too fat," I said. But she said nothing. "Rose?"

"Sorry." Rose said. She cleared her throat. "In your case darlin' it's quality you've got to worry about, not quantity. Now lookie here. Look at those two." *Law & Order* was just starting. Rose was watching a man and a woman in overcoats and scarves, the way people dress on TV. "They're happy as clams, they're on their way home to screw themselves silly but just wait. There will be a scream…" Rose paused. I waited. On the TV there was a scream. "Turn a corner and someone's dead." She clicked the TV off. "Why don't you have a couch in here?"

"I guess it would be nice." This was the first time I had ever watched TV in the trailer with anyone else. "I thought maybe I'd put a TV in the bedroom so I could lie down and watch it in there."

"Bad idea," chirped Rose. "Don and I put one in the bedroom, then we gave it away to Rory. Too many late nights watching whatever. English cop shows, Hawaii Five Oh. Seinfeld. Maybe you've got more self control."

Rose got up and headed for the back of the trailer. She turned on the bedroom light and made a clucking sound. "Now this is something: you actually made up the bed."

"When I was still in rehab, that was one of the rules." I went and stood beside Rose. She didn't comment on the clothes on the floor and stuff. She is about a head shorter than me and she turned and looked up.

"You know you're still pretty cute in your own funny way," she said. She reached up and ran a finger along the scar on the right side of my head. "A bit more like Frankenstein than you used to look."

I liked Rose and I liked standing close to her like this. We weren't on the job, there was nothing on TV and I couldn't think of anything better I should be doing.

Suddenly Rose put arms around me and pressed her head to my chest. "Do you still like girls Joey?" She looked up into my eyes. I could smell her breath and feel her breasts pressing into me.

"Uh…" I tried putting my arms around her, but couldn't get it right. Resting them on her shoulders was also no good. If I tried putting them lower, then her arms were in the way. I held my arms away from my body and looked down for a good place for them to land and put them back on her shoulders.

Rose pushed herself away. "This is nuts." She backed into the kitchen. "I gotta go home. I gotta meet the freezer guy at the plant at eight a.m." She was opening the kitchen door. "I'll see you then. Bring that lunch." Then she was through the door. "What you put into your body is very important."

"Yeah… thanks," I said. The door closed behind her and let out a sigh of relief. I was starting to get a hard on. I heard her car pulling out of the driveway. She beeped goodbye as she drove away.

I flopped into the armchair and heard a car crunching into the driveway again. By the time someone knocked on the door I knew it wasn't Rose.

She came in—the angry woman.

"Was that Rose who was just here?" she said. "She beeped at me." She swung a shopping bag onto the counter. "I brought you some mayonnaise. That stuff in your fridge is gross."

42. Heat

Last summer when the season ended, Rose kept me on with the cleanup crew for a few days. This despite the fact that I needed extra supervision, then even moreso than now.

When it was all over I stood by myself in the empty finger-packing room, the tables stacked in a corner, the floor dry for once, the smocks washed and folded and stowed away with the hairnets and the latex gloves.

Without music or voices or the gush of running water the place had a special silence. But all those echoes were still imbedded in the walls. I could feel the weight of all the prawns and herring and dogfish and the other creatures that had been iced and parceled, parceled and iced in that room until all their fear and anger was stilled. After a few minutes alone I lost my nerve and got out of there as fast as I could.

Noisy places have this going for them—that the noise pushes back against the ghosts, even though like echoes of past sounds, they are still there. They still circle us, watching. This is something I have always been aware of but there was something in Walter's story... something I've never actually *known* until that moment at the table in the Legion.

It's easy to get scared in the bush when everything goes quiet or on the road in the evening, with no cars in sight and the sun going down. However, there are also bright, noisy places where it's not good to be alone. At the fish plant, next to the big ribbon door, out on the loading dock there is a shack built onto the side of the plant. The compressor room.

When he is on the job, Jag spends a lot of time in that room and if Duncan is there they go in and out with tools and parts, shouting to and from the trucks, voices tense and fed up.

It is the only place I know in Pender Harbour that is always hot. Compressors blow heat out into the air and fans blow and roar and crash to a halt and are fixed and roar into life again, trying to keep up with all the heat that the prawns give up as they die. There are times when the air around the loading dock shivers.

With a dolly full of plastic cages I push through the ribbon door into the big cold room with its cement floor. We empty them into the sluice box and wash the prawns through the grader. The prawns ride down between the rollers. The little ones fall through first into net bags that are spread mouth-open over milk crates. Then, as the V-shaped space between the rollers gradually widens, the bigger ones and then the very biggest fall through, all the time washed along by cold seawater. We scoop up the net bags, dump them in fresh water to make the prawns dopey, then dip them in the chemical that was mixed up at the start of the shift.

The prawns are still moving when we empty the net bags onto the stainless table tops. In fact, some of them still angrily flick their tails and nose spikes. It's all we can do to pack them into the cartons. We have to pack them the way the Japanese like them, neatly in a double row facing each other, two deep. How good a fingerpacker you are depends on how fast you can fill a carton, get the lid closed and move on.

But we are told there is hell to pay if word comes back from Japan that a customer has bitched about a messy carton. So especially if fingerpacking is going really badly, especially if the prawns are still flicking and fighting, there's nothing to do but dump the whole thing out and start over.

There is an art to packing prawns. Take a prawn in each hand, spikes facing inward and place them in a row two by two on the bottom of the carton, vicious serrated nose spikes neatly overlapping. Then build another row on top. They give us a chart of how many prawns of each size will make up a kilogram—28 to 32 medium prawns, 24 to 28 large, and so on. Fill the carton, mark your number on the side with the grease pencil and weigh it on a scale—you should be ideally a hair over one kaygee. If you're a tad under and a buyer spots it, once again you and Rose and the whole plant are up shit creek.

My first year there, one of the women showed me that you can take two prawns in each hand when you're fingerpacking. I tried and tried but never really got up to speed that first year. The next year however, when thanks to Rose I was first hired and got my nickname, I got the hang of it. "Go Zero," the kids would yell when I got up a head of steam, grabbing four prawns at once. "Go Zero. Yo da man."

It is easier when the prawns just lie there, but if they are fresh off a boat or weren't kept long enough in the fresh water dunk, they can be a pain. Their powerful tails help them skitter all over the sea bottom, but up here it just makes them hard to handle, and gets them nowhere. Sometimes when I grade or fingerpack, one sticks me with its long nose spike and my flesh smarts and swells and it hurts like a bugger. But I have learned to forgive them. Not like some of the young guys with attitude, who avenge their honour by taking the offending prawn and throwing it on the floor and crunching it into paste.

The prawns feel cold to the touch, but I know there is so much heat in them. I am told that whatever moves makes heat, which is supposedly why you can start a fire by rubbing two sticks together. Prawns never stop moving. They chew up all the muck and mites and rot from the ocean bottom and, as they flutter around the undersea like moths licking the dark petals of their dead friends, it fuels them as they kick and scratch against the nets and cages and the traps we set for them. Prawns are so full of heat that they turn away from sunlight—they despise it and turn their backs and burrow farther down through the deepest waters where it's always dark.

43. The forklift

We hear a truck pull in and troop out onto the landing at the top of the stairs. It's the live truck with Barb at the wheel. I join the other workers unloading cages onto dollies, flinging great ribbons of water along the concrete dock as we transfer prawns to the live tanks.

I know that Rose feels bad about telling me I can't drive—that I can never drive the live truck. Then she calls out to us in our white smocks and yellow rubber aprons until somebody finds Derek, a young guy with bushy blond hair, and catches his attention.

"Take Joey here," Rose says, "and see if you can get him up to speed on running the forklift."

"We've gotta unload the truck," I say.

"The truck needs bait," Rose says. "See if you can get some bait over to the truck from the container. Derek will show you how to run the forklift."

"What about driving the truck?"

"Joey. It's not happening," she says.

"Why do I have to drive the forklift?"

"You don't have to. You don't have to drive anything. You can keep unloading the truck and then get back to work and not think about driving the forklift or the truck or anything except a hand dolly for the rest of the season."

We stand there in silence.

"Zero, this is your big chance," Derek says. "It's fun."

From the loading dock, I look back up at Rose but she is already gone. Derek leads me to the forklift.

"Get in, man."

I stand there taking deep breaths. "G'wan," he insists. "Get up on the seat." He leans over and runs through some of the basic dashboard stuff.

"This makes the fork go up and go down," he says. "No, don't touch that."

"I see the picture with the arrows," I say, "but it doesn't *feel* right. It feels like you should push it forward to make the forks go up."

"You don't," Derek says. "You pull it backwards."

"It feels like it should go forward."

"Godammit Zero…"

"Okay." I pull the lever back. The forks go up. I must have made a little sound of some kind because Derek says, "You like that don't you?"

"Uh huh."

"No, don't touch that. Now here: here's the hard part."

Derek shows me how to use the clutch to push and pull the gearshift lever to drive the forklift forward and then backward.

"That's the hard part," he says. "Now, when you drive backwards, here's the important thing to remember: always look behind you."

"I can look in the mirror."

"Maybe you can. I just get fucked up if I do that. I think you should look backwards."

I give it a try.

"No," Derek says. "Look backwards when you back up. When you're going forward, watch in front of you."

"Right. I got it." I fool around for a while picking up an empty wooden pallet, then putting it down again. Then I drive the pallet to the storage container and load up all the bags of bait I need. Then I drive the bait to the live truck. "Stop!" Derek shouts. I stop.

"You were too close," he says. "You almost lost your side mirror."

We unload the bait. Derek takes over and parks the forklift until the next time.

I thought my first forklift lesson had gone extremely well. But later I was cleaning up outside the door of the plant, under the upstairs porch to the office and lunchroom. Rose came out onto the porch with Barb and I heard Derek tell her, "Now I know why you won't let Zero take the truck. He's a real Captain Crunch."

I gasped.

"I don't know what I'm thinking," Rose sighed. "There's a lot of decision-making when you drive. More than you might figure." She stopped and I knew she was reaching into her pocket for a cigarette. But lately she had not been smoking her cigarettes. "He's got it in his head he wants to sub for you with the live truck."

"Oh if you gave him half a chance he could drive all right," said Barb. "But first he has to come with me down the coast to learn the route, and last time I let him ride in the truck the bugger tried to kiss me."

44. Scorpion

Jag pushes through the ribbon door, his truck still idling out on the dock.

"Looks like a faggot maternity ward!" He's making fun of the purgers and fingerpackers in their smocks and hairnets.

Wide rather than tall, Jag makes his presence felt among the women on the evening crew. Leering up at number one, Andrea: the tallest girl though only sixteen; number two Debbie, plump and just out of high school; number three Cindy who is Andrea's mother. Andrea seems to be good at ignoring him, Debbie looks up at him, shrinking back as Jag inches closer, and Cindy laughs and waves him away, get outta here. They all think Jag's gross, though the older women seem more able to put up with him. Some of them almost like him.

"In a place like this," Rose says, "you have to get used to all kinds." I'm not sure if she means the fish plant, or Pender Harbour overall.

I am now "on days" and hope to stay there. Duncan and I, and sometimes a younger guy, usually Derek, open up the place at 8 a.m. We put cardboard boxes together and line them with plastic bags. Mark them M, L, XL, XXL and Jumbo. Pull trays from the freezers and box up the cartons that got packed the night before. We put twelve cartons in each box, strap the boxes shut and dolly them into the big storage freezer.

We're doing this one Tuesday morning when a rumbling fills the plant and stops. Duncan looks out the window. "It's Jag," he says.

Jag has a new camper on the back of his truck. He gets out and so does his son Kyle.

"How you boys like it," Jag says, "my new vacationmobile."

Duncan and Derek say admiring things.

"Last day of the season we're off to California, the boy and me."

"If you don't get hung up at the border," Duncan adds.

"We can drive it in two days."

"Makin' a few stops along the way I'm sure."

Jag grins ferociously at Duncan and snorts. "Come on you guys, take a break for lunch. I'll take ya over to Garden Bay."

"Aw RIGHT!" Derek says.

"That'd be great Jag. But we got prawns to pack," Duncan says. "There's still cartons sitting right out on the table."

Jag immediately sees it Duncan's way. "You know, you're right. The prawns come first."

"Thanks Jag," I add. "But yeah, we got prawns to pack."

"You weren't invited anyway. I'm gettin' a window decal. No Retards Allowed."

Suddenly Duncan heads inside. Derek hangs around, before going in after him. I'm not too sure if Jag is joking. I point at his shiny belt buckle, in which I think I see a familiar shape. "Prawns come first around here," I say.

Kyle speaks up. "That's a scorpion, ya fuckin' retard." He spits toward the ground, but instead hits one of the shiny hubcaps on his dad's big truck.

45. Keeping secrets

Sandy jerked awake. Wolf eels ripping at her thighs, the water misting red around her. Escape blocked by banks of seaweed, rusted anchor chains, tangles of fishhooks snagged into her skin. The light from above dimmed, the eels grinned and down in the dark, ghosts and skeletons rubbed their bony hands together, waiting.

She rolled off the sofa. The doorbell rang again and she looked back at the couch's unbleached denim, stained with her sweat. She looked down to make sure she was decent.

It was Walter at the front door. "I was just looking at your picture," she said. Walter grinned.

Since Greg had left, Sandy was amazed at how many men dropped by offering to do odd jobs around the house or anything else she might need to help get her life together. She still had not figured out any reliable system to handle them. Each incoming man, who just happened to have his tools in the car, was a new challenge.

No tools were in evidence as Walter came in. He eyed the scuba gear dumped in the corner. Especially since it was mostly borrowed, Sandy hadn't wanted to leave it out in the car.

"Doing some diving?"

Walter sat down with a thump at Sandy's kitchen table. He and Sandy looked across at each other.

She gestured toward the scattered pictures on the tabletop. She had forgotten how tired diving made her. As soon as she had returned home she had made herself a coffee and started to go through the few photographs she had of Joey and Arden. Fatigue caught up with her and she lay down, just for a minute.

"There's the band," said Walter, pleased. He picked up the photograph of the country band, him and his accordion in front, Joey back a bit with his guitar, two rough-looking characters on bass and drums. A tattered gillnet formed a backdrop. "Gary and the Gillnetters," Walter said dreamily. "After Gary left and I took over the vocals."

"You want some instant?" Sandy said. "I have to get going soon." She had booked herself into the four-to-nine shift at the store to allow for her dive trip. Stupid, she thought wearily, though God knows I need every penny.

"We had some good times," said Walter. "A little while ago I tried to interest Joey in his old guitar. I tuned it and put it in his hands, but he didn't know which way was up."

"And there's these." Sandy handed over more pictures.

… Joey and Arden at a picnic table at Irvines Landing. Sandy remembered how pissed off Joey was that they could bring food from the pub but not drinks. Greg, not above conjuring a mickey of vodka from his vest pocket, was bearing up better. But it was the women who were trying to make the outing work: Arden with her dreamy smile, Sandy with the camera. *Now say cheese you miserable lot.* There were so many problems even then, but Sandy couldn't stop herself: she thought of that time more and more as the great days, when they were all so happy.

… Joey and Arden in the driveway of their little rented house on Warnock Road. What would they ever do in that place if they had kids? Once again Arden's smile, Joey grinning like a game show host. No wonder Sandy had followed him out from Saskatoon, she thought. Such a charmer, always an upbeat answer to everything. "Dontcha get sick of thirty below?" he said. "Come stay with us!"

He had made it sound like such fun. Greg, who had lost his favourite drinking buddy when Joey moved west, was not hard to convince. Finding work had been hell, but finally both Sandy then Greg got on at the lumberyard. For years they'd managed to get by, but lately Greg had been frustrated. Pender Harbour didn't offer many chances for a man to move ahead to a better job, or even sideways to a different one. "At least in Saskatoon," he'd grouse, "there was always opportunities."

Walter pushed the photos away. "That brother of yours is sure a blank slate. When I had him out fishing I'd hoped something would twig his memory and some of his old self might start to show, but..."

Dammit, life *had* been happy then. Arden worked at the supermarket and Joey worked odd jobs. They seemed to get by. She and Greg settled in at Skookum. Things were stable. Then one rainy Thursday Arden turned up missing and Joey turned up brain-damaged and everything went to pot. Now, just as she was getting used to being surrogate mom to her now thankless and stupid older brother, Greg heads off to the greener pastures of a younger woman and the big city. Just as she's getting used to being single, these old bones bob to the surface. Life just won't stay put the way you want it to. She glared at Walter as if it was his fault.

"I went scuba diving in Revenant Bay this morning. Joey and Arden's car is there. About forty feet down." She sank onto a chair opposite Walter.

"You're kidding me."

"Nobody knows it's there—I guess—except me, and now you."

"What are you planning to do about it?"

"I don't know," she said. "What if the cops decide that Joey killed Arden, and they lock him up? What if he *did* kill Arden."

Walter shook his head. "I just don't see it."

Sandy relaxed. "Me neither." She was starting to accept Walter as an ally.

"He wasn't a perfect husband—not that I'm one to talk—but he loved Arden. Everybody could tell. And if he ever had a nasty bone in his body, I never saw it."

"But they found him…"

"I think the two of them had the bad luck to run into the creeps who robbed the credit union. Joseph managed to survive, Arden didn't. That sounds more like it to me."

Sandy banged the door shut behind Walter. So much for keeping secrets—though she trusted Walter to keep his word and not tell anyone about the car in the bay. Walter had got what he wanted, which was a date to come by and look at Sandy's roof. She had suggested he could come on his own when she was at work, but he had gallantly refused.

Walter and Judy had been in the harbour for thirty years—Judy could often be seen driving up and down the coast tending her circle of quilting groups, bowling leagues and book clubs, while Walter fished herring in spring and prawns in summer, did odd jobs in the off season, held forth at the Legion and filled occasional engagements on accordion or piano. He was always letting on to various Harbour women that he was interested, and some he actively pursued. As to actual trysts, affairs or one-nighters—well, in a community this small, news travelled fast, but the field between rumour and reality was rife with gossip, ghost images and static.

She felt alone and needed someone on her side. If that someone turned out to be Walter, did that automatically move her up on his list of potential conquests? Walter was a likeable guy. Even his wife still liked him. But Sandy wasn't sure she wanted to be on his list. She thought of the pool of available males. Younger: the swampers and dogsbodies at the lumberyard, some of them not long out of high school if they'd even finished. Her age: the bachelors, hopeless but still-willing, with strong backs and pot bellies who deckhanded all summer, and all winter did odd jobs and collected pogey. The older: grandfathers, red-faced and weatherbeaten, who had married young, raised families and now were widowed, divorced, or one way or another lonesome and at least in their own minds, still virile and attractive.

Well, if she had to be on someone's list, it might as well be Walter's. She could handle him. Despite everything people said, his reputation included being a good man with a hammer. She wondered if she could get Christof to give her a deal on materials, how much Walter would charge to re-roof her place.

46. We the living

Rose coughed, "Joey, don't get that stuff in your lungs." She coughed some more.

By now I've mixed a lot of chemical. It's something I'm good at, and it is a job that doesn't bother me. Whereas just saying the word *lungs* makes Rose cough.

"I blast it with the hose," I said, "and stand downwind."

"You mean upwind."

Jesus Christ. "Whichever way the breeze is going…" I thought about that for a second, and tried to picture it in my head. "… I try to stand over the other way."

"Don't fill up the tank above that line, or the chemical will be too weak."

"Don't worry."

"And it's full of chemicals."

"I suppose that's why we call it…"

"It's preservative," Rose said.

"I know, Rose," I said. "I know it's preservative. If it's preservative, maybe it's good for you."

Rose butted out her cigarette in an ashtray. The rest of the types at the plant never miss a chance to flick their butts into the ocean. Rose carefully extinguishes her smokes. Then she dumps them all in the garbage so they will all end up at the dump.

She coughed and said, "Preservative is what you use on dead things. It does no good for we-the-living."

Okay, I had been trying to make a joke but… oh, the hell with it.

47. Whiskey Slough

Do you have any idea of the chances I took on you?

Wrapped in white bark, there is a tree that leans out over Whiskey Slough, the tips of its branches dangling its little cones like lures over the water, and on a summer night I swam under it when the tide was high. It was the season of jellyfish. They brushed against me in the darkness, too young to sting, gentle and uncurious. All along the shore the jellyfish swam through the branches—the blackberry and salmonberry bushes, the cedar and the apple trees—that reach down into the water. Jellyfish are powerful creatures. They trust themselves to the ocean—it is the ocean that decides where they go and how they live. The light shines through them and they gather it in their blood and seal it within to hold up against the dark. They are too slippery to get caught on those branches but I am not, the branches poke and scratch me in the dark so I swim away into the deep water.

It's a miracle that we're not all in prison right now.

Summer nights I leave the trailer and follow the road's curves to the dock at Whiskey Slough. Among the crisscross of floats there is a place where, because it's night, I can hide my clothes and slide into the water. Out in the slough there are rafts and moored boats where I can grab onto an anchor line and rest. It is deeper there, and in deep water you can look down and see glowing shapes—many creatures there glow with their own light—but in the shallows, even if the creatures are beneath me, their glow is hidden by the reflections cast by the lights onshore.

It's a miracle that no one's found those wrecks down at the bottom of the bay.

I look up at those lights and hear dirty jokes, grownups yelling at their kids, Shania Twain on the stereo—the sound carries out over the water—arguments, last-minute orders for pop, videos, potato chips, ice from the store, better get your ass in gear or they'll be closed. Once, a woman was drunk and I heard her sobbing—the problem, she cried, was that she had nothing, and that no one gave a shit.

It's a miracle that you're not in jail for life, and me too.

When I hear too much sometimes I swim out farther, out where the dark water swells up from the deeps and pushes its chill into the shallows. That's when it gets scary, when I can feel that this is not just a saltwater pond, but a whole ocean that, just offshore, deepens miles down into a dark that reaches the world round. Again I will rest on an anchor chain, or swim back into the warmer water, until I'm ready to pull myself onto the dock and rejoin the lights onshore.

I was almost at the dock when I heard the voice. I try to be silent when I swim at night in the slough. I hear so much, and I don't want people to think that I'm eavesdropping on purpose. I had swum in from the deep water, so I clung to the dock trying not to gasp.

There are people walking around who know everything, but no one is talking. Joey Windebank claims to not remember anything.

There was another voice there, a muttered, subdued voice. It spoke but I heard nothing.

Derek's not talking either. I know that. He's a good kid. I appreciate that. But what if her body floats up somewhere.

This was Jag's voice. And he was not talking loud. He was in the boat right above me. And that other voice, barely-heard. That was probably Kyle.

They can identify anyone now. Ya never heard of DNA? Things could change. Things could go bad.

I want you and some of your buddies to harvest everything that's ready and dry it and clean it and bag it. We'll triple-bag everything. Rip out all the insulation in the walls of the camper and layer it all in there and drive it down the coast. We'll come home and lay low. Everything legit.

I need to reduce the amount of stress in my life.

I needed to get far away from this boat. It would be dumb to pull myself up and walk along the float. So I started to swim around. I knew how to paddle quietly through the water.

I don't want any more of your—

Water splashed up my nose and I coughed.

Everything went quiet in the boat and then the cabin door slammed open.

I took a deep breath, closed my eyes and dove under the hull.

Just a few feet down the water was colder. I righted myself under the boat and felt barnacles scrape my shoulders. My head thumped against the hull. I couldn't see much except for a yellow glow that darted through the waters around the boat. They were sweeping the surface with the beam of a flashlight. From underwater I could hear the thumping of feet on the wooden float. I had to breathe so I pulled myself under the boat and up the other side. I came up under the float next to Jag's boat. I tried to be quiet and took deep breaths, not shaking the water out of my hair and snorting it out my nose like I usually do.

"You don't need to tell me that. I know the difference between sound that carries across the water and sound that's six feet from my fucking nose."

The light shone along the boards above me.

"There's nobody here." That was Kyle's voice.

Jag harrumphed.

"Dad, we're okay."

Jag stomped along the float toward the shore. I started to relax. My breathing was quieter. I thought I could stay there, clinging to the bottom of the float, until they gave up and went back on board. Then Jag came clomping back along the dock. When he got close enough Kyle said, "Probably just a seal."

"I found something up there. Get back on the boat," Jag said. "Wait for me." Without asking any questions Kyle got on the boat and Jag headed back toward the ramp.

Then everything went quiet.

Jag, I figured, must have got some notion in his head and gone up the ramp to the shore. From where I was under the float, I couldn't hear or see worth a damn.

I started to paddle along the float toward where I had left my clothes, following the dim underwater glow between the boats moored on either side. I could swim there in a minute in open water, but I pulled myself from one float to the next in slow motion, not wanting to dunk my head, come up gasping and have Jag hear me. In the shallows, once more the jellyfish began to bob in the water around me. Finally I got to the float's end— under the shore, in the shadow of the overhead dock, where I had stashed my clothes. I stopped and listened.

Somebody farted right above my head. The wood of the float creaked as a heavy body shifted position. Jag was up there waiting. He had found a pile of clothes and he was waiting.

I was scared to face him. Where could I go? I retreated one float back, swinging like a monkey from joist to joist so I would be farther from Jag.

Not far from the dock was a raft that boats sometimes tied to. I could swim to that raft—but I didn't know how quietly I could pull myself up onto it, and if Jag shone his light there, he would see me.

But I couldn't stay in the water much longer. I was getting cold. I thought of pulling myself up onto a boat, finding one with an unlocked cabin where I could hide, but I was afraid of Jag hearing me or seeing me. In fact, I was getting afraid to make any sort of move at all.

I left the dock and started to dog paddle toward the head of the slough. Every sound from the shore, a burst of music, the roar of a car engine, every shout or laugh that kept Jag from hearing me, I welcomed as a life saver.

Whiskey Slough is not very big and I never thought this would be such a long swim. Finally I was a hundred feet from the head of the slough where houses ring the shore. I felt my toes churning up the bottom mud. Oh shit. The tide was going out. Soon this would be all mud flat.

When the water was waist deep I tried to stand but there was nothing solid under me. I sank to my knees in mud, my shins scratched by broken oyster shells. I could feel my feet being sucked down. How deep was this mud? From the feel of it, bottomless. I struggled free and kept swimming, swimming in mud, coughing it out of my mouth and nose. Then I dragged myself through it like a salamander, bits of shell and gravel grinding into my chest belly, dick and legs. I pulled myself up onto a concrete boat ramp. It was dark so I stood, naked except for a coat of mud and oyster shell, and looked back to the dock where Jag waited beside a pile of clothes that no one was coming to claim.

48. Crimes past

Walking to the plant the next day it came to me that this, in fact, could be what the ptero—I mean the herons—were warning me about.

I jogged part of the way to work then gave up. I am tired today, I thought, and I will be even more tired later. At the plant I went around the feed container, to the side that faces out to the harbour, and leaned over to reach under the corner. The key was there and I went to open the door to the plant. Jag's truck was in the driveway and the door out to the loading dock was already open. From inside the ribbon door there came a voice: "Yer late."

I looked at my watch. Two minutes to eight. "The doors are open," I said. "I thought…"

"I'll tell you what ta think," Jag said.

"I gotta do boxup." I headed into the prep room where we assemble the cardboard flats into boxes. Jag followed me.

"Duncan's back is acting up," I added, pulling out a block of flats.

Jag followed me. "I can tell you what to think," he repeated. "No problem there."

"There's h-h-hardly any prawns now." I pulled out a handful of plastic liners.

Jag pulled at my hand and clear plastic liners spilled onto the floor, slippery as jellyfish.

Usually I partnered on the day crew with Derek and Duncan, but one afternoon as the season was slowing down Rose took me outside. She had a pack in the pocket of her smock, pulled out a cigarette and twirled it in her fingers as she interviewed me.

"You think you could do boxup by yourself tomorrow?"

I shuddered. "I think Duncan could do it better than me."

"Duncan's back is acting up. He's taking a few days off. But we only need one guy anyway. There just aren't enough prawns."

"Derek could do it."

Rose shook her head. "My new rule is, no one under the age of thirty does anything here on his own. Derek's a good kid as they go, but if one of his bipolar attention deficit pothead cokesniffing buddies drops by, they'll step out for a smoke and next thing you know, the evening shift gets here and nothing's ready."

I couldn't think of anything more to say and Rose kept working on me, twirling her unlit cigarette until little threads of tobacco twisted out onto the concrete. Soon I gathered that no matter how gently she seemed to solicit my opinion, she didn't much care what I thought about doing boxup on my own.

I crouched on the floor to pick up the spilled liners.

"I see you wore your gumboots inta work today."

"I need them."

"You should just leave 'em here. Like everyone else. Go home in your regular shoes."

"But gumboots are my favourite shoes," I said.

Shivering, wearing only a stiffening crust of shit-stinking muck and oyster shells, I had crept up the nearest driveway until I got onto the road. But I was surprised at how much traffic there was along Francis Pen Road on a summer's night. At the slightest hum of engine or flicker of headlight, I would dive off the road into the bush. It was dark and those bushes are full of blackberries and other wild and vicious prickles. Finally I made it to the school bus stop at the end of my road.

Back in my trailer, I took a shower. Muddy water spilling out onto the floor when bits of oyster shell and seaweed clogged the drain.

I only had an old pair of leaky gumboots and another pair of jeans that were too big. I had gained weight in the hospital but was again now skinny. I put on some socks—carefully because my feet were now scratched up, why does this always happen to me?—and found a shirt. I left the trailer for the second time that night and started to walk back to Whiskey Slough.

Now Jag was quiet. Was it possible that, whether or not he had it in for me, he had never paid attention to what I wear?

"I thought you'd wear running shoes," he said.

"Not me." I lied.

"Yer not some peeping tom, are you… who slinks around the harbour at night eavesdropping, peeking in windows."

Jag's boat was still tied up at the Whiskey Slough dock, but his truck was gone. I stood in the shadows near the dock, listening to the creak of the floats until I felt sure that Jag was no longer standing watch on the float. I walked down the ramp to the water. Something was floating there and I reached down and picked it up and shook the water off it. It was one of my shoes.

I took my one wet shoe and quiet as I could, walked down the ramp to the floats. It was late and everyone had gone to bed.

My clothes were gone. I searched the dark water but couldn't find them or the other shoe. I had lost it all.

Jag gripped me by the shoulders and pushed. I had to back up to keep from being pushed over, back up until I was right against the wall.

"Are you as dumb as you act like you are?"

"Why are you hassling me Jag?" I sputtered. "I got work to do."

"You don't remember me? You don't remember my son?"

"Lemme do boxup."

"Whaddayou remember, Zero? Do you ever wonder if you were anything other than Rose's pet retard?"

"I don't. I just don't." I kept sputtering and squirming.

"Ever handled a gun Zero?" Jag put one hand around my throat and pushed. This made it hard to breathe. I got scared.

"You remember your wife?"

I reached up with one hand and grabbed Jag's wrist and pulled his hand off my neck. It was hard to do—Jag was strong and he pushed back. But I had the wall to brace me and managed to do it. He pulled away as if I wasn't worth his time.

"Speeding ticket? Dope deals? Assault and battery? Ever done a bank job, and wasted somebody who got in your way?" He laughed.

I got nervous thinking about Blair's ThinkPad. Maybe Jag knew how much I'd wanted it, how I would have bought it if Derek hadn't stopped me. Maybe Jag knew.

"I just don't..." I began to sidle sideways, away from him so he wouldn't pin me again. "... I just don't know what you're talking about."

I slipped on a spilled liner. Jag grabbed my arm.

"Ever think that maybe I'm a nice guy. That maybe I'm trying to help you?"

That had in fact never occurred to me. I tried to shake out of his grip.

"Ever think that maybe one of these days, you'll start remembering?"

I just looked at him. He turned and stomped out of the room. As I cleaned up the spilled liners I heard his truck starting up outside.

Rose came by a couple of hours later and asked why it was taking me so long to get through boxup.

"No reason," I said. "Jag came by."

"And…?"

"Nothing," I said. "We didn't do nothing."

"*Anything*. You didn't do anything."

Soon I filled the last of the boxes and loaded them into the freezer. Rose sent me upstairs for more latex gloves, to put out for the fingerpackers when they came.

In the storeroom I turned on the light, went inside and searched the shelves. I tucked the boxes of gloves under my arm. Suddenly I felt very tired. I leaned against the shelves and felt the grey-painted steel cool against my forehead. I read the word stamped into the edge of each shelf, stamped and repeated again and again along the lengths of the painted steel. COMMANDER.

49. A very rare experience

"This is not good," said Walter. He watched the little cruiser approaching from up the channel.

"Quick." He handed Sandy a floater coat. "Don't let him see you're wearing a wet suit." Sandy put on the coat and crouched behind the gunwale.

"This guy's a fisheries inspector. He comes out with me sometimes to check the prawn stocks. Look for berried—uh, egg-bearing—females, and so forth. But I think we can pull it off." He waved as the smaller boat came alongside.

A short, bearded man called to them from the cabin window.

"Doing some sport fishing Walter." He nodded at the small scotchmen, not much bigger than party balloons that bobbed alongside the *Medusa Deep*.

"Hey there Ted," Walter called back. "Yeah, it's a test set."

They bantered back and forth. Sandy relaxed, realizing that Ted was not on Walter's case about regulations. He just wanted to gab. She flashed a big smile when Ted waved at her.

"Who's your friend there?" he asked Walter.

Sandy called out her name but Walter was already answering for her.

"A tourist from the big city of Madeira Park. I'm introducing her to the joys of prawn fishing."

"Let's haul'er up," said Ted, "and see what she's got."

"What?" Sandy realized they were talking not about her, but about Walter's alleged test set—a line with just a few traps on it.

"Just set it this minute." Walter shook his head. "We were going to watch the sun go down and then try our luck. I'll call you if you'd like a report."

"No need." They talked a few minutes more. Ted suggested Walter take him up Hotham Sound before the season ended. Then he started his engine and continued down the channel, dead slow for the first hundred yards so he wouldn't hit them with his wake.

Walter breathed a sigh of relief. "Let's get this over with."

There was more of a current this time. When Sandy hit bottom, silt stirred up from around her feet, but it quickly wafted away down the channel, and she had to work at holding her position. She removed the lead weight from the guide rope, attached it to the second rope and tugged hard to jiggle the scotchman on the bay surface. Walter saw her signal and started feeding down more rope; she could feel the hum of the winch as she pulled it under the car's rear axle and tied the end to the second rope. Then came the dark length of the tow rope. Once she fed it under the axle she pulled on the scotchman again, and swam back a few yards from the wreck.

What was taking him so long? As soon as the tip of the heavy tow rope broke the surface, Walter was going to tie it to itself to make a huge loop. He had rigged a pulley system to distribute the weight.

"This thing better not bust up my boat," he told Sandy. "But when it takes the weight, the safest place for you to be is down in the water. Stay well away from the car."

Finally the towrope went taut. The bay shuddered with the vibrations of the *Medusa Deep's* engine. Sandy had drawn a little picture of where the wreck sat on the bottom, and they had checked it against Walter's nautical chart.

From where she stood weightless, stabilizing herself with waves of her arms, the bay shuddered, the *Medusa Deep's* propeller turned the surface into a ceiling of foam, and the wreck remained unraised. Sandy had to stop herself from swimming over and giving it a push; there was no chance that her flippers would get any traction against the slippery bottom.

And then the car moved. It turned onto its nose and Sandy saw it slide away from the boulder, make one last languid turn towards the light before it was swallowed into the cloud of silt stirred up from the bottom. She swam to the signal line again and pulled on it, to confirm to Walter, if he was watching, that their plan was working. To stay out of the silt she swam into the darkness of the deeper water just past the boulder.

Arden's car left the bottom and swung out into the dark. *The trunk*, Sandy thought, *I never checked the trunk*. She swam forward over the dropoff and heard the roar of Walter's engine subside. As fast as through air in this slow-motion world, the car dropped out of sight. Walter had cut the rope. Uselessly she swam forward over the abyss.

I'm sure there was nothing. Was there?

Farther down the slope something caught her eye. A long dark shape. She cleared her ears and swam farther down, and then farther. It was deeper than Arden's car had been, yet still hadn't made the full descent to the channel bottom. Sandy shone the flashlight on it, but she was still too far away.

It was a pickup truck. Then she saw another dark form emerge from the shadows. *Don't tell me there are TWO pickups down here.*

The shape started to ascend towards her.

Now this is getting weird, Sandy thought. A pickup truck—she caught a flash of colour—with green headlights, and it's drifting UP from the bottom…

And she froze, even though as soon as she did she felt the current pulling her farther away from shore. Those weren't headlights. They were the eyes of the biggest shark she had ever seen.

Its tail waving as idly as sheets in a breeze, the fish rose out of the darkness and was coming towards her. Numbly, Sandy shone the light right at it. Its eyes glowed—never had she seen anything so bright and green. The curved slit of its mouth was like the chute of a waterslide. She could see herself sliding right past those rows of teeth to its cold belly.

Then a few yards from her the fish turned and passed her by. The grain of its leathery skin close enough to touch.

Sandy shook off her inertia and kicked away toward the shallows. Too scared to look back, she watched the bottom come closer and closer. Ahead she saw the base of the rock wall. She turned herself upright, but it was no good. The water was still too deep for her to climb out. She looked back. The fish was nowhere to be seen, but it could reappear any second, and there was plenty of depth for it here. These shallows weren't shallow enough.

Only one thing to do. Sandy set out swimming as fast as she could for the dock. Now, even here in the belly of the little bay, the water seemed infinitely deep and dark. She didn't look around, she didn't want to see anything, she swam just below the surface thinking, *I don't want my problems to end this way.* She almost screamed when one of the dock's piles, barnacled and waterlogged, loomed before her. Finally she surfaced, groped for the end of the float, and pulled herself towards the middle where the timbers sloped to meet the bay. She kicked herself up over the edge, and rolled gratefully onto the bare wood.

As she handed the gear over the gunwale to Walter, he proudly related his topside adventures. The sudden pitch in the deck as the boat took the weight of the car. The groan of timbers. A fraying strand from the towrope. A curl of smoke from the straining winch motor. The sway of the *Medusa Deep* under the car's weight as he swung it out of the shallows and over the deeps. The moment of victory as with the flash of a well-honed fish knife he cut the towrope, sent Arden's Toyota into the deeps, and pulled the severed ends back on deck.

Sandy didn't hear a word. Still encumbered with gear, she collapsed onto the deck. "Let's go home," she said numbly.

"I'd rather pilot from inside the cabin," said Walter.

"Okay."

He hesitated, waiting for her to make a move, then shrugged, untied the boat, jumped back onboard and went into the cabin. Sandy stayed slumped on the deck. The engine revved up and they headed back down the channel toward Pender Harbour. Then Walter was leaning over her. "You need a hand?" She let him help her up and guide her into the cabin.

Sandy felt like she had put a rope over her shoulder and towed the car into the deeps herself. Walter seated her next to him and put a towel over her shoulder.

"I saw… I ran into a shark down there."

Walter raised his eyebrows.

"A big one," she continued.

"Gave you a bit of a scare?"

She shook her head. A bit of a scare. "It came right at me. As big as this boat."

Walter scanned the horizon and steered farther out into the channel. Sundown was coming and at this time of year, it was easy to be surprised by pleasure boats racing close to shore. He cleared his throat self-consciously.

"This boat's a 37-footer. So a shark of that size is highly unlikely. Unless it was a whale shark, which in shallow water close to shore, is also highly unlikely. Also…"

"Okay, half the size. As big as a pickup truck." So much seemed to have happened underwater in a very short time. It was all getting mixed up in her head.

"How many gill slits did it have?"

She laughed hoarsely. "You are fucking amazing. I'm lucky to be alive. It was so close I could touch it. It was a shark. I did not count its gill slits."

"Sandy, I'm just trying to…"

"It had big green eyes."

"Aha. Then it was a sixgill. That's what I was getting at. A big one you say?"

"Jesus Christ Walter."

"Then you were in no danger. Sixgills are not aggressive sharks at all."

Sandy was silent. Walter cleared his throat.

"They stay in the deep water, and start up into the shallows around this time, late in the day."

Walter's information was not making Sandy feel one bit better. "I think I'll head back and change."

"You just had a very rare experience."

She closed the door to the cabin behind her and found where Walter had stowed her clothes on a bunk. It would feel good to get out of the wetsuit and towel off. But first, she thought she would just sit on the bunk for a while.

50. The cough

Whatever grudges Jag had against me were growing rather than fading with time. And just when I needed her the most, I seemed to be losing Rose.

After she came to the trailer, Rose was not the same. She would just not talk to me like she used to. If I asked where to put away a tool or some new stock, or if I took too long to bring prawns from the live tanks to the grader, Rose would say, you know where that goes or, better get your brain in gear, mister and sometimes she would just sigh and look away. I started to worry. What had I done. Did it mean she would not be calling me next season? This could be bad.

Some nights, once I came home and ate, I would turn around and walk back to the plant again and join the evening shift on their coffee break. We would sit together in the growing dark, outside if it wasn't raining too hard, in the circle of patio furniture on the edge of the loading zone. If I volunteered to work during these visits, the word was always no. Lately, Rose had stopped coming to sit at the picnic table circled by grimy plastic chairs.

"She doesn't want to associate with us smokers."

"We're a bad influence."

I heard someone coughing up in the lunchroom. I took a deep breath, got up from the table and started up the long flight of stairs. Rose was in the lunchroom gripping something and giving it one of her hard looks she uses on creepy guys in bars. At first I thought she was waiting for an important call on her cellphone, but she was looking hard at a pack of cigarettes and trying to suppress a cough. She raised her eyebrows skeptically when I came and sat beside her.

"I'm trying to quit," she said.

"Once I tried to start smoking," I said. "But I got nowhere. It just made me cough."

"No kidding."

I told Rose something personal that I thought I would never tell anyone.

"I think my wife used to smoke."

"Yeah?" Rose looked at me funny. "Is that something you remember?"

"I guess so." Actually I had a memory, one that sometimes came up clear and sexy, of kissing a woman whose mouth tasted of cigarette smoke, but I was embarrassed to tell this to Rose.

"Not that I knew her that well," said Rose, "but I believe she didn't. She wasn't the type. She was more the grow-your-own broccoli, eat-your-granola type. And look where it got her. No offence Mister Zero but that's life. You can walk out in the street…"

"Maybe then, it was because of cigarettes that something bad happened to her."

"Well," Rose shook her head, "I guess that's as good a theory as any. But to get serious, Joey—no one knows for sure, but don't let anyone tell you that any of it might have been your fault. Probably you were nowhere near Arden when whatever happened to her happened. Maybe it was her idea to go away and disappear and never come back. Nobody ever found her or evidence of her and nobody came forward so maybe no one will ever know for sure. Maybe it was an act of God, and nobody can take the blame."

"Still…"

"What I mean is, it's the same as these cursed things." Pronouncing it cur-sid, rattling the pack of cigarettes like a broken toy. "Like I was saying, you can walk out in the street and get hit by a truck. And you're just as dead. Oh what the hell." Quick as she would tail a prawn, Rose pulled out a cigarette and the second it was in her mouth a Bic lighter appeared in her hand. I didn't say anything about no smoking in here—she knew that better than anybody.

Rose lit the cigarette, took a few quick puffs and tamped it gently into a saucer. I got up and poured myself a coffee. I asked Rose if she wanted to come and sit outside with us but she looked away. As I went downstairs the women around the patio table looked up at me and I stopped on the stairs, all of us listening to Rose up in the lunchroom coughing.

51. Blood and pain

I keep my eye on Jag as we unload bundled flats of cardboard boxes, bags of bait, coils of rope, scotchmen, plastic tubs of fish oil… we load his truck up with garbage and old cardboard boxes and he is away again. The stuff he brings in, it is up to us to stow it in the tool shed or the big steel storage container, but sometimes when Rose goes to get some rope or bait jars to sell to a fisherman, she finds supplies mysteriously gone. As well as having a share in the plant, Jag does his own fishing and makes his own deals.

Rose would get pissed off earlier in the season, but now she shrugs. "That guy is a bundle of sidelines. All totally legit I'm sure. Whereas me, I'm only supposed to be running this place."

Towards the end of the season, as our numbers declined, I seemed to always be working with Jag's son, Kyle. He had looked so sad the night I came back to the plant. Jag getting Rose to hire him back didn't seem to cheer him up. In fact nothing seems to get him going. Kyle is big and heavy and when he is in an especially bad mood, he is like a circus bear who, costume or not, really wants to bite somebody.

Whenever Rose told me, I would help Kyle with what he was doing. Once downstairs we were unpacking bundles of cardboard—flats that we would have to make into boxes—and all of a sudden Kyle yelled fuck. A bundle had slipped out of his hand. He wiggled his hand and blood slapped onto the floor.

He came up to me. "Look at this."

The cardboard had sawed his hand open all right. It seemed to me I had cut myself like that before, but I couldn't remember what to do. The skin ragged along the edges, and blood pushing its way out. I made a face, then looked away and kept working.

Kyle followed me and shoved his hand at me. "Look at this fuckin' thing!"

He had me cornered. "Must hurt," I mumbled.

He snorted. "I've cut it way worse than that before." He headed out the door, dripping blood. "I can handle it," he said, and I heard him on the stairs outside, stomping upstairs to get Rose to bandaid it up. I took a break from the cardboard and went to get the mop.

52. Commander Zero

I dump a cage full of prawns into the sluice box, and they are whipping their tails and scrabbling with their spider legs, blocking the channel that washes them onto the rollers of the grader. But one of them holds back and crouches in the basin, watching. While I'm breaking up the jam I see a movement out of the corner of my eye, though by the time I take a real look, there's nothing.

The hidden prawn has made a break for it. Hooking his brittle legs over the steel rim and rolling as he hits the wet concrete below. From the floor he calls to the other prawns—

"Look at this guy. He is spaced out or just slow as mud. This is our last chance to escape the evil machine and those like him who serve it. We can't save the others but we can save ourselves. Jump my brave friends jump!"

—and as I look away, pushing prawns into the channel, over they go, a double handful of them. It is a long way and the floor is hard. Swack! Ouch!

Their tough shells leaving them unsquished, the brave sea creatures roll to their feet and join their leader under the salt spray of the grader, where he is waving his feelers defiantly. The air burns him inside and out, it is hot and vibrates with death but he calls, "This way my friends." The prawns hop and hobble after him through the ribbon door. "This way I smell the sea."

"Hey Zero!" Duncan yells from the packing table. "Yer losin' yer product!" A few of the girls call out, "Zero! Zero!"

Outside the sun has gone down, but its dryness and heat still rise like a cloud of poison from the concrete loading dock. The prawns hate this. Out in the dry night air they won't survive for long, but here the saltchuck smell is stronger.

"Do you hear that," the prawns cry. "Do you hear what they call you our leader? Zero! Commander Zero!"

With awful speed a huge shadow lurches out of the ribbon door. The prawns hurry toward the edge of the dock, following that ocean smell. "This way my friends, my sisters," yells Commander Zero as they scuttle under the white-painted rails and drop off the edge. The human dives for the last of them but *snap*, a twitch of its sharp tail, the monster is outmaneuvered and the brave little creature is free.

Under the white-painted rail, splashing into high tide. Commander Zero flicks his powerful tail and shoots down to the bottom, past the starfish and oysters at the tide line. Into his belly tubes he sucks the rich gracious salt water. Alone he loves the lovely cool and the dark, diving deeper, colder. But he is alone.

Above him the prawns struggle and scream as the dock sharks attack from every side. The eager little fish pull off their legs and seize them by the tails. Zero smells the clean saltwater blood of his brothers and sisters, but the water is also clouded with red fish blood, as the prawns fight back, slashing and piercing with their serrated tails and their sharp tusks. He charges up toward the light. His snout sticks into a soft white belly. His tail whirls and thrashes. The dock sharks are chickenshit little fish scared—unlike us—of darkness and death. They sob and flicker back under the float to hide.

Some of the prawns drift, twitching and legless into the dark. The ones who can still swim follow their leader down. Some of them are bleeding. There is a swirl of shadows, a flash of white mouth and a dogfish scoops a prawn and vanishes.

All around them are rock cod, wolf eels and octopuses, but Commander Zero leads the prawns out to the mouth of the harbour, deeper and deeper until they find a quiet place on the bottom where they can rest.

"Come my brothers, my sisters," Zero says. "Come and we will escape deep to the sea. Where it is most cold and dark, down deep where they will never find us. Deep in the forgotten cities, Atlantis for example, that lie down there. Never forgetting the lessons we've learned. Those black net things like basketball hoops, they're bad news, we won't go near them, and when the stupid octopuses and snotfish get pulled away in them, we'll throw back our heads and laugh. Deeper and deeper our people will spread, along the deep gutter bottoms of these black inlets, and when the stupid humans blow themselves up or die of sars or bird flu or global warming or whatever. Yes it will happen, even with all their traps and ropes and freezers they are big fucking retards, stumbling around up there in the light. Sure they own the world, but someday the world will end for them and when that world ends, still we shall prosper."

Commander Zero laughs and one by one the prawns stop being afraid. They have traded certain death at the fish plant for their superdangerous everyday life. One by one they follow their leader down into the dark.

"Zero," Duncan yells, "yer product." He leaves what he's doing and stoops next to me, reaching under the grading machine and bringing back a big blurry prawn. "This one's made a break for it." He tosses it onto the rollers, sees it get washed down and through into the XL basket.

"I guess I was daydreaming," I said. "Sometimes I wonder what all this is like… you know, for the prawns."

53. The guitar

"Learned to run a forklift have you? Joey you were a mysterious character—even before you got your bump on the head. Only back then you told funnier jokes and—do you remember?—you were a hell of a guitar player."

Now alone at home I opened the long black box that has shadowed me for months from a corner of the trailer. I stood the guitar up on the bed then held it in my lap the way I'd seen people do.

I touched the two thinnest strings with my fingers. They made bright, chittery sounds. It was the way I imagined the prawns talked if we could hear them. Then I touched the two thickest strings with my thumb. Now *that* was a prawn boat: the rumbling sounds their diesels made as they idled at the float, the chucka-chuck of the gensets, the rattle of the winches. I could hear that in those two thickest strings.

The guitar also had two strings in the middle that I didn't really know how to deal with.

I snapped the guitar back into its case and walked down to Francis Peninsula Road. A fisherman on the way to the plant picked me up. I couldn't remember his name, just that his boat was the *Midnight Clear*.

"You goin' on tour Joey?"

I explained that I was thinking of trying to get back to being able to play guitar like I used to. When we pulled into the plant I showed him and explained about how the thin strings were the sounds the prawns made and the thick strings were the sounds the boats made. He just made a face. We went up to see Rose.

It wasn't Rose there, but her son Rory. Don, her husband was there too, talking into the phone about as quickly as Don can talk.

"Hey Joey… Lloyd…" Rory said.

"Joey here claims he's back playing the guitar," said Lloyd, "but what he's actually come up with is the biggest damn crock…" Rory asked me to hand him the guitar and strummed it a couple of times. "You ever tune this thing?"

I rubbed my chin. "It seems to be working okay…" I babbled, envisioning "tuning" as making appointments with high-priced experts like car mechanics.

Rory shook his head, played one of the low strings, then the string next to it. He fussed with the pegs on the end of the guitar, then strummed his hand over all the strings and handed it back to me. "I had to guess at the 'A,' but at least now it's in tune with itself."

I touched the strings again. Did this sound any better? I sighed: more shit to learn. "What's the charge for that?"

"Can you play my Christmas carol?" asked Lloyd. Rory and I just looked at him.

"*It came,*" sang Lloyd. "*A prawn. A midnight clear…*"

"G'wan," said Rory. Don came off the phone and joined us. "Where's Rose?" I said. "I came here to see Rose."

"She's not coming in today," said Don, then he said to Lloyd. "I've got Barb coming in. She can probably handle the night shift, if Jag and Duncan put in more time during the days."

"So… where is she?" I asked.

54. Men will be men

At the Legion I found Walter out in the smokers' tent with some fishermen. I told him that Rose had left the plant.

"She's *what?*"

"I asked Don," I said, "and he said they're trying to keep her at home…"

Walter swore and looked deep into his beer. His glass was getting towards the bottom.

"…for as long as possible." I added. I pulled up a chair and fit it into the table next to him. I would try something I had been afraid to try before. Joey, I said to myself, don't screw this up. I groped in my pocket and brought out some money.

"I guess that means," I said, "that she's getting better, and will soon leave home, and come back to work."

"I doubt that very much," said Walter. He sighed. "Goddammit. You know Joey, sometimes I think life is like trying to swim across the Georgia Strait out here. You start out all together with your family, your friends. You figure you'll all make it across no problem and that the whole thing's going to be one big happy picnic. But the more you swim, the more the people around you start to fall away. You try to rally around with whoever's left, but one by one the swimmers up ahead of you disappear, and one by one when you look behind you, no one's there either. And it's just a matter of time before whatever got them, gets you."

There was not much I could say to that. I looked at the scattering of bills and change in front of me. I raised my hand to get Janice's attention.

"I've always thought the world of that woman," Walter said, "and Don of course, is a hell of a good guy."

"Joseph, I haven't seen your hand up since the old days." Janice was there with her tray. I looked at my money.

"I would like to get Walter another beer and myself one as well please." I looked at the money on the table.

"And she's devoted to Don," Walter continued. "God knows Rose has had occasion, a number of times over the years, to make that point clear to me."

"And of course, there were those stories going round about you and her." Walter leaned closer to me. "To be honest my friend, I could never blame you for a second. Although your late wife was also one heck of an attractive woman, and she was a beautiful person to boot, it's like they say: men will be men."

Janice set the beers in front of us. I straightened up. "Is this enough money?" I asked.

He spread his arms. "And look at this. Our Joseph has bought a round." He raised his beer and clinked it with mine. "Next you'll be back smoking up the place on your guitar."

"I was playing it just yesterday." I said.

55. The woman in the woods in the night

Soon, I found that I was asking Walter if he wanted to leave. He said maybe so, then he turned back to who he was talking to.

"And I won't hear you say a word against your wife you bugger." Gord Mackie was telling him. Gord is a big slow guy, but it sounded as if he was building up a head of steam. "That woman, in my opinion, is a saint, and she's been putting up with you and your goddam bullshit…"

"There's no need for you to swear at me," Walter raised his voice.

"And you don't hafta say insulting things that have no basis in truth."

Walter looked around. He spread his arms. "Gordon Mackie sir if we can back up, what the hell was it that I said?"

Gord took a deep breath. "It's not me that's the problem, it's my goddam chiropractor. I think…"

This was way over my head. It was getting late and obviously I would have to take care of myself.

I went to the washroom, came out and went past the bar to the front door. "Are you leaving us?" Janice said and I said yes, I think I'm going to walk home. "Take care," she said.

Outside it was cool, once I put some distance between myself and the heat generated by the smell of beer and cigarette smoke and the racket of TV and stressed-out fishermen. From beyond the trees that surround the Legion came the rush of a passing car and the mew of some bird or other that comes out late at night.

I took the back lane that goes from the Legion parking lot out to Lagoon Road.

Where the Lane joins the road, a pickup truck went past, heading into town. It appeared around the curve, I shielded my eyes, it slowed, its brake lights flashed, then it was gone.

I headed away from the town—it takes me a long time, maybe an hour to walk home. Headlights appeared behind me sending my shadow rushing across the trees. I stumbled away from the pavement into the weeds, and the truck I had just seen loomed behind me, and pulled over onto the opposite shoulder. The driver stuck his head out the window.

"Where the hell you been tonight?"

I didn't recognize him in the dark and I didn't know if he recognized me. Sometimes people are drunk or just mixed up.

"I said where you been goddammit." A car went past and he drew his head in, and couldn't talk until the sound faded away. Then he got out and slammed the door, engine still running, and came across the road.

"Where the hell is my wife?" It was Rose's husband Don charging at me, so that I backed up a bit.

"I've just been at the Legion," I said.

"Don't tell me Rose is down there!"

"No she isn't."

Don turned away from me and looked off down into the dark in case Rose was knee-deep in the swamp behind the Legion, peeking out at him from the bulrushes. "So you haven't seen her tonight?"

"I was just down there... down in the Legion. I haven't seen her anyplace else except the fish plant." Actually there was that time Rose had come to the trailer, but that was long ago, two weeks or longer. It didn't seem like a thing to mention.

"She's gone from the house." Don turned back to me. "Are you sure you haven't seen her?" The threat had gone out of him—he just sounded tired and scared.

"Do you think it's a bingo night?" I said. "Or that she's gone up to the Roost?"

"That's just it," said Don. "She could be anywhere. You know... she started on some medication. She started experiencing some pain. What with her condition."

"Her condition," I echoed, as if I knew what he meant. "That's too bad."

"The pills make her... anyway, she didn't take the car." Don drew a deep breath and looked around warily as if Rose, because of the medication, would
any minute burst hollering from the bush and run into traffic. "She's not driving. She's just gone out of the house. Wandered out."

"I'm sorry Don," I said. "I'm sorry I haven't seen her anyplace."

"This fucking medication." Don looked down at the pavement. The wind had gone right out of him. His feet dragged as he crossed the road back to his truck. As he fired it up he looked at me out the window and said something I didn't quite catch. He put the truck in gear and headed into the dark, out towards the peninsula's end.

I walked until I got onto Francis Peninsula Road. On the bridge over Canoe Pass I looked out over Bargain Harbour. On my right the sky still glowed pink, and on my left the lights from the city to the south washed the night out of the sky. It was dark only where I stood. Then the road went sharply uphill, I began to climb and the sky was closed in by trees and the slope ahead of me. It was getting late and there wasn't much traffic on the road.

When I heard a voice coming out of the trees, I had the impulse to hide. I have known kids to hide and make fun of me, calling out to me. I stopped, then I heard nothing. Wings whipped by my head—one of the big owls that haunt the peninsula's summer nights—and then out on the slough I heard the croak of a heron.

"Pterodactyl," I said out loud, and when I looked around, afraid someone might hear, a figure came through the trees, along a driveway to a house down on the shore. It was Rose, dressed in blue jeans and a sweatshirt.

"Is that you?" said Rose.

I said that yes, it was me and she stopped like a startled deer. I looked at her where she stood unsteadily on the side of the road. It was like she was waiting for me to go past. I walked a little ways and looked at Rose and she looked out into the dark.

"You know," I said. "You know Rose, you're supposed to be home."

"But I haven't seen anyone," she said. "I haven't seen anyone out here."

"I saw Don on the road. He's worrying."

"I was thinking about that story," said Rose. "But there's nobody in the dark."

It's true, I thought, what Don said was true. There is something different about Rose. Medication.

"You don't need any story," I said. "You just need to go home so Don can see you're all right."

"The story you told me. About that girl that Walter met, out in the bush."

Shit. Somehow this was going to turn out to be my fault.

"In the bush, at night. He encountered her. I thought what that might be like."

"Just a second Rose," I said. I looked both ways for cars and then I jumped into the bushes. I had been in the Legion for quite some time. I unzipped my pants and peed into a bush. Then I zipped up and went back to the side of the road.

"Rose?" I called. She was across the road, heading down the hill to Bargain Harbour. She paid me no mind. I called again and ran until I caught up with her. She still paid me no attention. Then she stopped and I ran into her from behind. She started to cough. It was a bad cough, ancient and dry, as deep and angry as the heron's cry.

When Rose stopped coughing she said, "I should go to bed."

"I can help you get home," I said.

"Take my hand."

I led her back up the hill, as we walked going slower and slower until Rose said, "I can't anymore. I'm just so tired."

I put my left arm around her back and scooped up her legs. Once I got my balance, holding her in my arms, we continued towards her house. Of course, by now she had walked halfway down the hill so I had to walk back uphill carrying her. I didn't do much talking.

"It's what Walter said, about that woman he met," Rose said, "that woman in the woods. I wondered if it could be true—maybe if they give you their kiss, the pain will go away." A car went by, blinding us with its lights. Rose shaded her eyes with her hand. As my eyes adjusted I could read the words on her sweatshirt: Penticton, BC. On her feet she wore baby-blue slippers.

"Anyway, that's what Walter said happened to him. But maybe for a woman—maybe I could become like her. I walked in the woods but nobody came. I think I need to go up the back roads into the hills. Up the mountain like Walter was."

At the top of the hill I told Rose I had to set her down. I tried to get her to walk but she just leaned against me. I was winded, panting like a dog.

"That Walter Conacher, he's full of it—full of shit"—she spat the word out—"in a lot of other ways, and like everybody he twists everything, the way things happen, he tells them in his own way. If you're a woman, he's always trying to sweet talk you. But I don't believe…"

"Here," I said. "I think I can keep going with you now Rose. Unless of course you feel up to walking."

That was no good—I couldn't get her moving so I took a deep breath and picked her up again. We were getting close to her place. I didn't see Don's truck in her driveway—he must still be out looking—but a car was there.

"…anyway, he might bullshit, but I don't believe he actually lies."

I set her down at the top of the driveway. "We got you home," I said.

She blinked at the car in the light from her house. "Jamie is here," she said. He is another one of Rose's sons. We stood out on the road and looked down the driveway at her porch lights.

"I think I'd like that vampire woman to find me," Rose said. "I used to like women, years ago, before I was married, and not just men. I was young and I liked everything"—she closed her eyes against the bright lights—"and sometimes a woman, if you get a feeling for her you know, she's just so beautiful."

"Do you think you can walk to the house?" I said.

"Just think, if her teeth were sharp enough, they'd feel almost gentle sliding into you, almost loving. And then you live forever. Walking the woods at night, forever. I could go for that."

She left my side first unsteadily, then getting back her balance. I was afraid that if I was seen bringing her home, Don would think I'd been hiding her all along, so I stayed there at the side of the road until she reached the porch and put her hand on the wooden rail. A woman came out and called her name. The sound of voices came from inside the house.

Rose?

Mom?

56. The blast freezer

Eyes shut in the coldest place in the world. It was pitch black and when I opened them it was pitch black still.

We treat the blast freezer like it's just another room, but it is not a room, it is a machine for sucking heat out of the living and it was sealed tight. No light came in around the door. I got to my feet and reached out—for a minute I reached out on every side and felt nothing, I felt alone on the dark side of the moon. A thousand miles away from the sun's light, then I touched something—it was the grid at the front of the fan. As I touched it, a little red light went on. Did I just do that, I thought. Just a tiny red ember in the dark. I didn't even think there was a switch there, I couldn't have done that, it must have been…

The fan started up.

It did not sound right to me, that cartons "slide off" trays and get lost between the racks. When we pull off trays for box-up we look carefully into the racks to make sure nothing gets left over. We always remember—because we are always reminded—how much one of these cartons sells for in Japan, that if the fishermen are getting six dollars a pound for their prawns, then somewhere in a Tokyo restaurant that's what they're paying for one single prawn. The lights are bright in the freezers. It's not like we can't see what we're doing.

In fact, the whole day had been weird. Jag had grabbed me the day before and told me we were starting "super-early." I would have to be there at 6 a.m. for box-up.

"The thing is, don't tell anyone. People are getting laid off every day. Guys will be pissed if they find out you're getting extra work."

It made for a weird way to start the day. Setting my alarm early and up at dawn, I got to work at six, and there were the steel fingerpacking tables, all dragged to one side of the room, and there was Jag.

"We got a different procedure today Joseph," he said. I waited to hear what that might be. There were not that many cartons of prawns for me to box up.

"We got to check the shelves," Jag said. "Make sure nothin's got left behind. Freezer by freezer."

"Left behind"—this did not sound very likely to me. But if Jag said there might be cartons back there, he is the boss.

I started at the top of the racks in the blast freezer and worked my way down. I didn't see any damn cartons. The racks are rolled right to the wall and they are made to exactly fit trays of one-kg. prawn cartons. There is not a lot of extra space for stuff to slip away and get lost.

While I looked, I kept the door open. I heard a motor start up and then, to my surprise, I heard the forklift rattle into the plant through the ribbon door. I was curious but figured whatever was going on out there, I would find out soon enough. Jag was an expert at finding tasks for us to do.

The blast freezer is the coldest freezer in the plant—even with the fan off it was cold. I had to crouch to look in the lower racks and even go on my knees on the floor. I wore lined rubber gloves and when I went on my knees I wished I had lined rubber pants.

If there were any cartons they should come out, I thought, because we would have to defrost this freezer soon. Today in fact, before the evening crew gets in. The floor was rocky with ice. At the edge of the racks next to the wall I saw something dark stuck in the ice, and I thought of the blackened bones of the woman in my dreams.

I was all that was left between her and life. Sometimes at night, I would dream her, and for a second I wondered if that dark thing, if it was her arm, if I was dreaming her now. My knees were freezing and I hurried along looking into the spaces under the racks.

"Find anything Zero?" I could hear Jag outside. Before I could answer the door slammed shut. Why the hell would he want to do that, unless it was one of Jag's famous practical jokes. I just kept looking—he would open the door up in a minute. But I heard something thud against the door, something heavy. Then the lights went out.

When the fan started up I backed up, hit the racks, and fell on my ass. I hate the wind from that fan. Even on the hottest days I wear a toque when I have to go in the blast freezer. It is so cold it scorches like fire. Now I had nothing on my head but my baseball cap. I squeezed my eyes shut so my eyeballs wouldn't sear and crack in that evil wind. When I tried to stand up, my rubber gloves stuck to the floor and they stretched and ripped when I pulled them away.

I groped to the door and pushed. It was stuck solid. I pushed and then I felt for the handle that unlatches the door. I had never known the door to be closed when someone is inside the freezer, but in case it ever happened there is a crash handle. If you push against it, the door opens. Even though it was dark and I was flustered and pissed-off I wasn't scared—not yet, because I knew about the crash handle.

I pushed on the handle but nothing happened. It was stuck solid like everything else in this fucking place. STUCK. I wanted to yell in a big voice like Jag's, but instead I pushed and pushed but it was going nowhere. Then I hammered it until my hands hurt and it still wouldn't move. I pushed on the door but nothing would move and I couldn't figure out how it would get stuck.

"BUNCHA FUCKUPS BUNCHA FUCKUPS," I yelled. "JAG LEMME OUT."

Scared scared scared lemme out out out. In the darkness something moved and I spun around, but there was just the little red light on the fan. The fan was blowing air at me so cold my skin cracked.

The fan roared, the voice whimpered scared scared scared lemme out. I could smell seawater and I knew she was there in the darkness in front of me, closer than she had ever been. I hammered on the door and yelled stupid shit like "The joke's over, you can lemme out now!" and I didn't know why Jag would not open the door. Maybe he had gone away. He would have to be back soon. It would have to be really soon. I waited for a hand on my shoulder, a hand dripping seawater that would freeze to my skin, and if I turned to look my skin would peel off, and I would see that the hand was just bones. Pretty soon I would be just bones too.

I dived under the blast of the fan, under the woman's reaching arms, and hit the wall and slid down at the base of the door. That's when I squeezed my eyes shut, and when I opened them, I saw her.

I saw her by the light of the blue flames rising from the floor, a hideous scaffolding of blackened bones, the tatters of clothing soaked and chewed by the sea and its creatures. I avoided her sightless eyes and looked away. The blue flames were heatless. My hand landed on something and I drew it away before the glove stuck to it. It was that dark thing I had seen before, now imbedded in ice, reappearing and flickering in the blue firelight.

I had kept meaning to move it, but like a goof I never did and now it was stuck. It was the crowbar I use to bust ice off the floor when we defrost.

The crowbar was in the ice, bedded down good. The floor burned my knees and when I jammed my hands in to grab it, my left wrist was crammed against the steel rack and I felt the skin burn. The steel was even colder than the ice. I knelt to reach in my pocket. My hands felt like two rocks in the sea, but I pulled out my pocketknife and pried the blade open with my thumb and began to chip at the hunk of ice. I chipped and chipped until I heard a little *nick* when my knife hit metal. I carved on each side of the *nick* sound, and felt the shape with my wrapped fingers. I couldn't get a grip on it. I began to shiver and a long shudder ran down my body. I had to stop until the shudder passed, tried to keep my hands from shaking so hard that I'd drop the knife. It is a little knife and would slip to one side. I kept chipping, huddling on the floor in a tight ball. Finally I could get my hand around the bar inside the ice but it was still stuck tight. I chipped some more, pulled, chipped some more. When I pulled again the damn thing came up off the floor, raining chunks of ice down my front.

I closed my eyes against the spray of ice and when I opened them inside the freezer it was black as night. I knew I was alone again.

Now I held the crowbar in my hands but couldn't move. My knees felt stapled to the floor. I flopped over to free them and came up dry even though she had been in there just seconds ago dripping seawater. It is so cold I thought, even the seawater, it freezes so fast. Scared, scared, scared because I would die if I did not get out of the freezer. I had the feeling that if the flames flared up again I would be lost.

I reached up with the crowbar and hooked onto the door handle and pulled myself up. Then I pushed on the door: nothing happened so I rammed the tip of the crowbar into the doorjamb and, like moving a dolly stacked with full cages, leaned into it with all my body weight. Nothing.

I couldn't feel my arms. There was ice on my face now and below that just pain. I pushed the crowbar again, prying against the door. *Crack.* The door moved. I pushed again. The door gave kind of a heave, but it would have to open soon, I was running out of strength. Then I dropped the bar, fell to my knees and reached for it, but this time I knew I couldn't get up. I tried hard again to fit it into the door. On my knees I leaned against the door and pushed myself up.

With the heel of my hand I hammered the curved end of the crowbar and it slipped into the door jam. I pulled, felt nothing, heard nothing crack or give over the roar of the fan. I pulled harder. A little tongue of light appeared at the top of the door. I pulled the crowbar back out a bit—I knew that the longer it was, the better I would be able to pry—and when I pulled again, the tongue of light got longer.

Suddenly it was big enough to shove my head through. I pulled some more and thought it might be big enough for me to crawl through. I grabbed the edge of the door and pulled myself up. My head went through the crack—it was so warm out there. I got my shoulders out... now I was getting tugged back inside. Where my clothes pressed against the freezer door, they were freezing and sticking.

But... the forklift was backed against the door. I grabbed onto the cab and heard my smock and pants ripping away from the ice. I pulled myself out of the freezer and fell onto the concrete floor of the plant. Then I tried to get up.

The floor felt warm. The light hurt my eyes. Daylight was coming through the windows, and I closed my eyes so that if the flames rose around me again, I wouldn't see them. Back in the freezer, the fan roared.

Keep blowing you fucker. I am free. I am outta here.

I pulled myself up onto the forklift and stumbled out through the ribbon door onto the dock. Rain was falling. I wanted to go upstairs and have a coffee, but how the hell to get up there? It was such a long way up. I ached so bad, my legs especially and my shoulders too. I leaned against one of the live tanks. The rain was warm for once, and so was the blue plastic of the tank. So much heat in there. I pulled myself up onto the lid of C1 and lay there in the rain.

57. Local fishers rejoice at Joey's survival

"YOU FUCKING WRECKED IT!"

Barb did not say anything. When it came to handling Jag, she was just a beginner. At a time like this, I needed Rose on my side.

"The whole season is FUCKED!"

"It's not my fault," I said. "I know how to go in and outta that door."

"Something musta gone wrong, Jag," Barb said. "Like Zero says, he knows."

"FUCKIN' RETARD," yelled Jag. "Fuck up our whole operation."

"You shouldn't call him that."

Jag gave her a look that made Barb back up a few steps. He turned back to me.

"You panicked in our goddam freezer and fucked up our door trying to get yourself out."

"I got shut in there. Someone out here screwed up, and it was not me." I felt suddenly calm. Nothing could get worse than what I had just gone through.

Barb said, "Now that's just silly. Why would anyone do that?"

"You can't lock yourself in," Jag yelled. "It's not possible."

"I'd be dead now," I said, "but I found that crowbar and pried."

"Five thousand bucks." Jag ran at me but I didn't back off. I stood where I was. He grabbed me by the collar.

"Are you hiding in there," he yelled. "Because if you are, you better stay hiding. You better stay a goddam retard, yer way better off."

"The forklift. It was backed against the door," I said.

"That's not where I found it," said Jag. "It was out on the loading dock. Where it's been all night."

We all looked at the door. We looked at the forklift. I didn't say anything. I couldn't think of any way to make things better.

"What are you guys talking about?" said Barb. Jag let go of my collar and looked at her.

"The last day of the season, I'm out of here anyway. I got better things to do than this."

Jag stomped out. Barb looked at me and didn't say anything. I wished that Rose was here.

58. The universal power of music

"Look," Walter said, "why don't we get together on this," so Sandy found herself driving to the last place she wanted to go.

"Why don't I come over..." he said. Sandy's mind raced and, for want of someplace better, she came up with the Legion.

She turned on the wipers. It was a blustery night—rain slapped against the car and as she approached the corner of Warnock Road, its lone street light went out. Climbing the hill, Sandy saw that the houses over Whiskey Slough were dark, here and there one flaring forth with a genset, another glowing dull yellow from oil lamps, another the harsh white light of propane.

She snorted: this would be a good night for Walter's vampire woman. In her headlights a figure would appear at the side of the road, sometimes holding out a thumb, then disappearing. She thought about the jumbled story she'd heard from the ever-credulous Joey. Who else but Joey, she thought, would be impressed by Walter's bullshit.

The power was out too in Madeira Park. At the end of the Legion parking lot she turned, not sure what she wanted most, to park or head home, and her headlights swept across a few shadowy pickups and the hot green sports car that meant Carla, the night bartender, was on the job. And there was Walter's pickup. He was in there waiting for her.

Inside, Sandy squinted and scratched her name in the guest book. The buzzer was down, so Carla came around from the bar and let her in with a sigh of resignation.

"I just closed the taps. You can have a bottle of beer if you want."

Sandy looked around. Tonight the big room was a maze of shadows and she felt scared to make a false step. Under the hard white glow of the emergency light over the shuffleboard, a tableful of people looked up at her. Sandy knew most of them as Skookum Lumber customers. Under the overhead glare they looked malnourished, angry and diseased—barking and joking bitterly over their beer and leftover fries.

Carla handed her a beer across the bar.

"Sandy," a voice said. "Over here."

"How's your brother?" said someone else.

"He's okay," she said. It was some young guy. She couldn't recognize his voice and all she could see of him, or anyone else, was a black shape against the emergency light. "A bit of frostbite. I can't even get him to take a day off."

One of the guys at the table was Kyle Jagges. "Our resident retard." Out of the darkness she saw Walter Conacher rise from his table.

"He was in an accident Mr. Jagges," said Walter. "And no longer has a perfect brain like yours."

Sandy kept her eye on his silhouette. "Is there a chair there Walter?"

Suddenly a light spurted up and she saw Walter's face flickering orange against the dark. She found herself a chair. "Walter, you know you can't smoke in here."

Carla appeared behind her and clunked an ashtray down on their table. "This is wickedly exciting," said Walter.

"Blackouts scare me." Carla was holding a cigarette herself. "I figure it's an emergency situation."

"The end of the world," Sandy said.

"Don't say that." Carla looked sadly at the table of people near the shuffleboard. "It's just that I like to be able to see what's going on."

"It's like the great days of the nineteen eighties are coming back," said Walter. He held the smoking cigarette in his fingers like a lottery ticket, a potential jackpot. "Now if we could just get back the big salmon runs…"

"I've been here once in the last eight or ten months, and I was with you that time too," said Sandy. "The Legion." She watched Carla's silhouette in the dark, a tall, bony woman with a pale face and red hair. She cleared the bottle from the next table where an old guy was snoozing and went back to the bar. Sandy waved a cloud of smoke away from her face.

"Are you going to smoke that whole thing?"

"Oops. Sorry. No, I ration myself." Walter delicately tapped out the cigarette and slid it back into the pack.

Sandy waved away the last remnants of smoke and leaned over to him. "Look, Joey talks to you. Has he ever said anything about what happened to him? The actual accident. Do you think there's anything he remembers?"

"Not a thing. And believe me I've listened for clues."

"Then why did Dan Jagges try to kill him?"

"I heard that was an accident."

"You can't have an accident like that in an industrial freezer. You can't lock yourself in. You can't."

"I heard that he panicked and couldn't get it open."

"Come off it Walter, you've been around those freezers, and you know Joey."

Walter sighed. "You might have a point. I'm starting to think that Joey's brain works just fine—that it's his communication skills that are fouled up. The ways that information gets in and out. Sometimes it seems to work, then the next second…"

Sandy humphed.

After a minute of silence Walter said, "Nobody denies that Danny Jagges can be a mean bugger."

"Is that why you're afraid to point the finger at him?"

"I'm saying three things…" he leaned over closer. "A: We should keep our voices down because his son's over there by the shuffleboard. B: It's no use accusing someone of something you can't prove…"

"Watch your language." Someone raised their voice at the shuffleboard table. "There's women at this table here." The guilty party said something and the watch-your-language guy stood up.

"Show some goddam respect," he said.

The swearing guy stood up and indeed Sandy recognized, in silhouette, the sulking mass of Kyle Jagges. *Punch your lights out.* The other man spat out an insult. Kyle, mysteriously, started taking his shirt off. The man next to Kyle got up and grabbed him and pulled him away as the other guy aimed a kick. The crowd was on the two of them like wasps on an apple.

"You guys grow up."

"Cool it."

"Why dontcha just…"

"I'll call the cab," Carla said.

"That girl," Walter said to me. "The girl at that table, Sandy…"

"What are you talking about?"

Where Walter pointed Sandy saw a pale white face, and long

black hair, then a figure loomed in front of the emergency light and cast a shadow over everything.

Evidently Carla's deferential bearing concealed an unyielding female authority that she knew would be obeyed by males of Kyle's ilk, even drunk and ready to fight. Sandy heard her, in a serrated whisper that left no room for dispute, tell Kyle he was too drunk to drive, to take the local cab or, to save her own job, she'd have to call the cops.

Kyle was not so drunk to miss the message that to piss off Carla would invoke a lifelong curse—a curse that in a town this small could spread beyond the Legion's four walls. He started doing his shirt up, heading for the door. A farewell was heard from the table under the emergency light.

"CHICKENSHIT FAGGOT COCKSUCKER."

The speaker's companions tried to shut him up; Kyle started unbuttoning and headed back. Carla told him to cool it, she'd phoned the cops and they were on their way.

Everybody knew that even if they were actually on their way, the cops would take at least a half hour to get up from Sechelt, more likely the whole night. The Sechelt cops, knowing that they had zero chance of getting to a brawl in the harbour while it was still happening, sometimes would not show up until the next day.

Still shouting threats, the other man left his companions and backed onto the dance floor where Kyle, now naked from the waist up, grappled him, both men snarling and kicking.

Walter stole a glance at the other table as the fight was breaking out. In the uncertain light Sandy saw only the pale round face and the long dark hair of the woman there. Then, as if shaking off a trance, Walter jumped out of his chair, swerved to avoid the fight, sat down at the piano and opened the cover over the keys. He started playing; some old jazz tune, Sandy thought.

People were grabbing at Kyle and grabbing at the other man. With his shirt off, Kyle looked soft and vulnerable as an enormous baby. But suddenly he was alone, walking unsteadily toward the door, and everyone was heading back to their seats. Walter finished the tune and stood up, carefully closing the lid over the keys.

He plopped back down across from Sandy. "Works every time," he said, rewarding himself with a sip of draft.

"I can see that I've really been missing out by not coming here."

Somehow, despite the darkness, the coming and going of the fight had cheered everyone up. Carla declared the taps re-opened. The emergency lights started to dim and Sandy peered at her watch. "I have to open the store at seven," she said. "What was the third thing?"

"What?"

"You gave me an a, b and c."

"Oh—C is that I'm not afraid of Jagges personally—but frankly, why would he want to kill anyone, least of all Joey. Danny does okay for himself around here. He's not what I would call a desperate man."

"That's an interesting word." *Desperate.* Sandy thought how vulnerable Jag's son had looked in the bad light of the bar. Reamed out by rage and self-pity.

The last table got up to leave. "I hear he runs a big grow-op up on Mount Hallowell," she said. Walter still had his eye on the pale woman with the black hair. "In fact I think I see a few of his field hands there."

"Really?" said Walter. "That dark-haired girl…"

"Sure," said Sandy. "They charge stuff to Jag's account."

"Really." They watched the party clatter out the door and the room fell silent. Now only Walter and Sandy were left. Walter looked over to where Carla was finishing up at the bar. "Jeez Carla," Walter said. "I bet you want to go."

"Actually, would you guys stick around till I lock up? I hate being here by myself."

"I thought Jag was bad," Sandy said. "His son is worse."

"If you ask me," Carla said, "we should legalize marijuana and we'd get rid of some of these bloody gangsters and their grow-ops."

"Grow-ops," said Walter. "Now this is all I'm hearing. Grow-ops. It's because we've depleted the fish stocks."

"But anyway," said Carla, "nobody's quite like the Jagges father and son. There's screwed-up genes in there somewhere. I won't go near Mount Hallowell as long as they're doing their agriculture up in the bush there. Pit bulls, guns, biker creeps. All the stuff I left Surrey to get away from."

"Mount Hallowell," said Walter. "Carla, who was that woman with them tonight. That dark-haired girl."

Carla said, "I don't know her name. She sure didn't stick around to look out for Kyle or anybody else when the shit hit the fan."

Suddenly the lights came on. The ceiling fans started turning, Carla headed back to the bar and her vacuum cleaner began to roar.

"...destroy the evidence..." she yelled as she sucked ashes from around the shuffleboard. "Or I'll be in deep doodoo."

Walter finished his beer but Sandy left hers. She took their bottles and glasses up to the bar. Carla rolled up the vacuum hose and counted the night's take.

"I didn't know you played piano Walter," she said.

"In music as elsewhere I'm a jack of all trades."

"It was the funniest thing," Carla said. "I'd just dialed the cops again when the music started up. I thought the power was back on."

"I recognize that tune," Sandy said. "I forget the title. A kiss is but a kiss."

"It's the universal power of music," Walter observed. "To soothe the savage breast. Whenever a ruckus starts in a bar I go to the piano. Though they're kind of a vanishing species. I'm glad this establishment has hung on to its upright."

"I always wished I played music," said Carla.

"Really? Well, you know I've done quite a bit of teaching, and I'd be happy…"

Carla and Sandy looked at each other and laughed.

"My offer is serious," said Walter. "It is the offer of a gentleman."

Out in the parking lot, they watched Carla lock up and head to her green MG.

"Nice car."

"The divorce," Carla said. "I earned every penny."

"Look, Sandy…" Walter said.

"I'll be lucky," said Sandy, "if I can hang onto my old beater. And the house."

They watched as Carla got in and beeped the horn as she drove off.

Walter said, "Look, Sandy…"

"Yes."

"You know, next week is the jazz festival down in Vancouver. I'll have the *Medusa Deep* docked down there."

"My goodness."

"I mean, if you want to come down. There's lots of space on the boat. We could take in a few concerts."

"You want to go to the jazz festival… with me?"

"Seems like you could use a break…"

Sandy laughed.

"And you know, there's no hanky-panky involved here… I just thought…"

Sandy kept laughing. She hadn't had a good laugh like this in a long time.

59. Revenge

There was a lot of noise about me being fired etc., but Barb pleaded my case. With the season ending, she pointed out, she needed experienced guys to help with cleanup. The totes and hoses will be drained and cleaned. Then we stack the totes up out of the way. When that happens I plan to take over the forklift and show Barb and everyone a thing or two.

Today the last boats are coming in and their few measly cages of prawns will be processed and fingerpacked and frozen. Some of the fishermen have quit already, but most of them hang in there, if they're lucky catching enough to pay for fuel, hoping that at some point they will get a bonus day with lots of prawns—a day when they will make more money than it costs them to keep the boat in the water.

Meanwhile as we all know, today Jag is taking off. He is at the plant having a meeting with Barb, both of them on and off the phone to head office in Vancouver.

Jag's silver pickup, sporting its new camper, is in front of the plant. If a fisherman's truck comes in to unload we will have to work around him. Straight from the plant today, Jag has let us know, he is heading for the great USA and then to Mexico. It is warm there with palm trees and cheap to live, better than here Jag says.

Upstairs in the storage closet, we are down to our last box of latex gloves just as the season is ending—this is how carefully

Rose ordered everything. I lean down for it and I see that word again stamped into the edge of the steel shelf. COMMANDER. It is stamped into the metal every few inches. When I step back I see that word all over the shelves.

Jag will be gone by the time the evening shift arrives at four. I drag the little tote outside to mix the chemical. There is a mask and this time I use it. Rose is in the hospital they tell me, and that is scaring me, so I hook the mask around my head, even as I fear that they will make fun of me. I pull out two bags of the chemical and drop one of them unopened into the tote. The other one I slice off the corner in the usual way and pour it in, blasting it with the hose. When I am done the chemical is ready.

The full bag is floating. The label is good and wet now and I look around to see if anyone is watching as I pick up the bag and peel off the label. Then I hug it in my arms like a pet bunny and scrape off the last bits of glue with my pocket knife as best I can. Since the freezer incident the blade is bent and rusting. Finally I put the knife away and use my fingernails on the last of the soaked label.

I'm getting nervous as I dry off the bag with a length of brown paper towel. But I have done an okay job. It's become a plain plastic bag full of white powder. I shove it into my coveralls under my apron.

I am nervous and I look around a lot. No one is at the office window? No one is hanging around the live tanks or down on the floats? Then I take a deep breath, walk out to the back of Jag's truck and stuff the bag into the space between the back of his camper and the tailgate.

It is a present for Jag. He likes people to know he is around, and once the guys at the border find this bag of nameless white powder, they will pay him lots of attention and his truck too—probably search every inch of it. We will see who is the goddam retard around here.

60. Sechelt

One of these days... I think and the woman says "What?"

"What?"

"One of these days what?" she says.

"I guess I was talking to myself." We have passed Trout Lake and are driving down the long hill into West Sechelt. Up to now, the highway has gone mainly through trees. I look out at the trees spreading their branches into the light. Through the window I could hear them, their long unbroken sigh of relief that we're just passing through.

People are always telling me I should have a plan. Those people would be happy to know that at this moment, to myself, silently I am planning.

"I was just coming up with a plan."

"What sort of a plan."

"I'm thinking of getting a pickup truck."

"That's great, Joseph." The woman snorts in disgust. "Good luck. You'll need to take a driver's test, you know."

"What if I found my old license?"

"God help us all."

"At work, I was getting good with the forklift."

"Your licence is probably expired by now—wherever it is. No one's ever found any of your ID, and after this long a time, to get a replacement licence, you'd need to take the test."

This scares me a little bit. "Are you sure?"

"I checked with the government," she says.

I wonder if she really checked, or if this is a lie. This woman does not want me to drive. "I'd pass the test just fine."

"Driving takes a lot of decision-making and common sense," she says. "Let me know how it works out. Maybe you can start driving me around for a change."

Now we see the ocean on our right, and clouds lowering over the dark line of Vancouver Island. We come out of the last grove of trees onto the bypass road that goes around downtown Sechelt.

"Anyway," I say. "I'm going to talk to Rose about this."

"What on earth for?"

"Maybe when the next season starts, in the spring, maybe I can do some driving for the plant. Like drive the live truck."

"You're going to bring this up with Rose *now*?"

As we drive I can see that the woman is scanning the back of the mall for a parking space. We pull in.

"I don't have much time," she says. "Come on."

She takes me in the mall to the florist's shop.

"You should buy Rose some flowers," she says.

"I just wanted..."

"Joseph, you should really bring some flowers or chocolates. At least a card—she'd really like that."

"That's not what I was planning."

In a burst of fury she snatches up a small bouquet in a vase and opens the card on the counter.

"Here," she orders. "Sign this."

There's such an edge in her voice that the woman behind the counter looks away from us, and I immediately lean down to sign my name to the card.

We drive up a street to a part of Sechelt where I've never been and pull up in front of an unfamiliar building.

"For getting home, you know the bus times," she says. "I gave you the schedule. You've got your watch. If you miss the bus, get to the highway and stick out your thumb."

"Why aren't we at the hospital?"

"Because Rose isn't there. She's here."

I take another look at the place. There's a little sign. It looks like some kind of motel.

"So... Rose isn't sick?"

"Jesus Christ."

I can tell that if we stay together she is just going to get more pissed off. I open the door and she says, "Rose is very sick. Don't start asking her for favours. She's already done everything she can do for you."

Now I'm out of the car, so she gets out too. "This is a hospice. Rose is in palliative care." She glances at her watch. "Do you know what that means?"

I don't.

"It means you're not going to start talking to her about what she needs to do for you next spring." She starts circling the car, and I back away. She reaches back in and gets the flowers I left inside.

"It means she's been sucked dry by people telling her what she needs to do for them, and ordering her around and asking favours and not even noticing that she's fainting and gasping and coughing up blood." She shucks the vase into my hands like a football and I fumble to keep from spilling the flowers all over the parking lot.

"It means this is the last ride you're getting from me. Now get in there and be nice. Don't be an asshole. Think about Rose's needs." She circles back to the driver's side. The woman and I look at each other over the roof of the car.

"Do you even remember my name?" She yells. "Every little grunt in the fish plant or the lumberyard you can call by name, and you treat me like I'm the fucking ghost and I'm not a ghost. You goddam basket case stupid fuckhead. *You* are." She gets back in the car and I stand back. "YOU'RE THE FUCKING GHOST."

61. The torture option

As she pulled out of the parking lot to head south to the ferry, Sandy relished her new independence and maturity and tried to squelch the feeling of having stomped on a helpless small animal that was only looking to stay safely in its cage. She glanced in her rear view mirror and glimpsed Joey standing in the hospice parking lot, lost, lonely and hapless. She bit her lip. The thing about Joey, she reminded herself, is that things work out for him. The thing is, somehow he'll find his way home.

Meanwhile she was going to spend the weekend at a jazz festival—not the little local one but a real big city one with, well… whatever jazz festivals had. She was hoping for black guys playing saxophone, some singers—singing actual lyrics, not just going scoobie doo yabadaba—and not too many wanky guitar solos and synthesizer nerds.

Staying with Walter on his boat, according to him loaded with spare bunks, seemed to be a plan that could turn into what they called in Skookum's customer service workshops a "situation." But she considered herself a master of situations and she would cross that bridge when she came to it.

Look at me, she thought, making things up as I go along. Finally a few days of adventure—just enjoy yourself dear. The ghosts of the past, the Harbour and all its fuckups and losers and hopeless cases and hothouse flowers fluttered happily through her brain. You all have a good weekend too, she thought.

A huge silver shape loomed in her rear view mirror on the approach to Davis Bay. It was Jag, tailgating her so tensely that she glanced at her watch to make sure she wasn't running late. Then there was a break in the oncoming traffic and the truck roared past her down the hill. There was still tons of time, and no need to catch up to Jag in his great big hurry. If he and that sullen mutant son of his were going to be on board, it was a good excuse to stay in the car during the crossing. They were embarking on their vaunted California trip. Sandy would not be running into them at the jazz festival, or anyone else from Pender Harbour. She had moments of dread that out of all the million or two people in Vancouver with all its streets, buildings and byways she would somehow run face to face into Greg. Not likely, she soothed herself. It would take a lot more than culture to lure him downtown from the Skookum main yard and the Burnaby sports bars and shopping at Metrotown with Ginny.

The bank had taken out her mortgage payment at the end of the month, and the account still hadn't bottomed out. In fact, she was hardly into her overdraft. Maybe I'll do this, Sandy thought. Maybe the chicken and rice stir fries, heavy on the rice, and no cable TV will pay off. I will actually make it. Greg or no Greg.

At the ferry terminal she pulled into a boarding lane. Out on the sound a log boom sauntered past islands green in the sun, and far across the water the white peaks shouldered halos of cloud. A young man with a backpack and a handful of shopping bags came towards her through the parking lot, scanning the rows of cars, and when Sandy shut off her engine she looked up and his eyes met hers. Glancing nervously over his shoulder, he trotted up, calling her name.

Her mind raced. She remembered this kid helping his dad slide two-by-fours into a rusty minivan. The other bits of his identity clicked into place. He had even worked in the yard a year or two ago, but she hadn't seen him lately. Think Sandy, she thought, think.

"Derek," she said.

"You got some room?"

He put his luggage in the back—a school backpack and two plastic shopping bags, one stuffed with a sleeping bag.

She said, "I can take you downtown."

"Great." Derek didn't look at her, but kept nervously scanning the parking lot.

"Taking a holiday?"

"Got work up country," answered Derek. "Taking the bus."

"Whereabouts?"

"Up country a ways." Which could mean any place from the Fraser Canyon to Inuvik.

Sandy could see the ferry in the distance. The weekend was starting and the boat was already running late. It would arrive in ten minutes and then would take at least another ten minutes to empty and start loading the Horseshoe Bay traffic.

"Probably a good thing," Sandy observed, "to take a break from life in the Harbour."

He looked at her sideways. "Well… things are getting kinda hot there."

"Too many tourists," Sandy said languidly.

"Too many assholes," said Derek. "Things are getting weird in the harbour. There was that accident at the fish plant—Zero, well ya know, Joey Windebank got locked into a freezer and almost bought it…"

"And it's so sad about Rose," added Sandy. "I just dropped Joey at the hospice in Sechelt so he could visit her. Could be the last time, I guess."

"Jeez," Derek said. "You and Joey. I forgot you're related."

There was a long pause. *This kid knows something*, she thought.

"There's the ferry," Derek observed limply. "Maybe you should start 'er up."

"They need to unload first." Sandy had a thought. "You know Derek, I actually spend quite a lot of time taking care of my brother, and of course nobody really knows what kind of trouble he got into, that made him the way he is, but sometimes I think that some people in the harbour know a lot more than some other people."

"I guess… I guess he can be pretty high maintenance," Derek said blandly. "Sometimes I think he only gets on at the fish plant 'cause of Rose."

"That's just what I mean," said Sandy. "And sometimes—though I don't have any right to feel sorry for myself—sometimes I feel it's especially hard on me. I mean, I'm the one who goes over to his place, almost every day, and makes sure he's eating right, and cleaning up after himself."

Derek seemed to think about this. "Yeah," he said. "I guess so."

"After all, I still love the guy, and he's my brother, even if he doesn't seem to think so. And I think that considering he's my brother and all, that I'm entitled to be let into the loop. I mean, it would help me, and I'm trying to help him. Don't you think that's true?"

"Uhuh."

God, this is nauseating, she thought. And it was getting her nowhere. She saw Jag down at the vending machines and decided it was time to tighten the screws on Derek.

"Oh look Derek, there's Danny Jagges. Let's call him over."

"Jesus Christ no."

"Why not—you know Jag don't you? We can all hang out together till the boat comes in."

"Jeezus no," hissed Derek. "If he sees us together I'm toast."

"Who—Jag? Now why would that be?"

"Look, I'm just trying to get outta here. I got a friend who knows people can get me jobs that pay cash under the table. I want to stay off the radar for a while."

"But Derek… why would you need to do that?" Sandy added. "Oh Jag's coming this way. Maybe he'll share his cheesies." She put her hand on the horn. "I'll honk and get his attention."

"Jeezus…"

Sandy beeped the Escort's horn. Heads turned in the car in front of her. Sandy grinned and waved with both hands—sorry—goofy accident. Derek squeezed down in his seat, trying to fit under the dashboard. "No kidding. He'll kill me. For real."

"Here's the deal. You can stay in the car and try to keep out of sight until we get across. Then I'll drive you to the bus station and look the other way while you head up north and go off the radar. Just answer one question."

Derek's head was still under the glove compartment. "I don't have anything Jag wants to know."

"Jag's gone. I'm messing with you. Sit up." Derek sat up and looked warily out at the lot.

"Revenant Bay," said Sandy. "Something happened there."

"That's the question?"

"That's it."

"You won't tell anybody?"

"You can trust me."

Derek looked out at the incoming ferry. Its wake drew a white arc across the sound as it approached the huge timbers of the loading ramp. "They got pushed into the bay," he said. "None of us thought we'd see them ever again. They both went down into the water."

"Wait a sec. Who?"

"Kyle did it, with the truck he stole. We stole. Joey's wife was driving their little Toyota. That was one big truck—they never had a chance."

Sandy stared numbly at the ramps lowering onto the ferry's parking decks.

"The whole idea of robbing the credit union—that was Kyle's idea. I already knew Joseph… Joey… from the fish plant, and I got him into it. He took a lot of persuading, but he was broke. But the farther we got into planning it, the more Kyle took over, and soon the whole thing was out of control. It's Kyle who screwed it all up. Loaded guns, that was Kyle. Bringing in his dad, that was Kyle. Otherwise, it would have been a quick snatch-and-grab."

"Wait a sec—Jag is part of this too. You guys are the ones who robbed the credit union?"

"Well… yeah. Yes and no." Derek closed his eyes to think. Cars were thudding off the dock and racing up the lanes toward the stoplights. Thinking completed, Derek opened his eyes.

"It went like this. Kyle convinced Joey and me that we could rob the credit union and drive away with bags of cash, and no one would get hurt. That if we stashed a boat at Revenant Bay we could take the boat back into town, just as if we'd been out fishing the whole day. Kyle knows how to
hotwire trucks, so we could get a vehicle. But for a boat, Kyle got his dad and his fishboat."

"This is bullshit," said Sandy. "Jag is not stupid. He covers his ass. He would never get involved in such a dangerous, loser scheme."

"Kyle lied. He told his Dad we were hunting elk. The story was, we'd cut it up on the shore and needed a boat to get away with the meat and antlers—a boat with a freezer for the meat. Jag loves that kind of outlaw shit. He'd shot an elk already up at his grow-op and got away with it. He said he knew where he could sell the antlers and the meat too."

"So Jag didn't know what he was getting into."

"Kyle figured once it was a done thing, his dad would be proud. We stormed the credit union on that Tuesday morning in our ski masks and camo and they started packing all their cash into bags. If there was a problem it was Kyle. When he fired his gun into the ceiling, it freaked out everybody, 'specially me and Joey."

Dammit, I should have helped him. Sandy thought of Joey standing in the parking lot. I knew they were always broke. But so are lots of people in the harbour, I told myself. None of my business. Like hell.

"Outside of that everything went smooth. We knew there were never cops in the harbour on a Tuesday morning. We figured, when we got to the highway turnoff, that we might get lucky and no one would see us head north. We'd scoped out the road to Revenant Bay. When we got to the end of the road we could see his boat heading in to that old dock.

"The only thing, there was someone else too. Joey's wife had got wind of the whole plan, I don't know how. She was standing there yelling at Jag, who was completely baffled. She started yelling at us, yelling at Joey—'I know who you are,' she yelled, 'take off that stupid mask and you can still walk away from this.'

"'What the fuck is going on?' Jag yells at Kyle and Kyle turns red.

"I already could tell, without even seeing his face, that Joey wanted out as soon as Kyle had shot off his rifle. I didn't blame him—our guns weren't
even loaded and Kyle said his wouldn't be either. If you pull this shit with a loaded gun, things can really go bad."

"Uh, Derek. Robbing people is really bad to start with. Loaded gun or not."

"Do you want me to keep going?"

"Sure. I'm just going to look out the window here. So I don't have to look at you. But I'm listening."

"When he sees his wife, Joey turns to us and says, 'Guys, trust me on this: my lips are sealed.' Then he strips off his ski mask and the camo jacket, Kyle all the time yelling at him and goes to get into the car.

"'You can't fuck off on us now,' yells Kyle.

"'That gun wasn't 'sposed to be even loaded,'" yells Joey. He gets in the car.

"But Kyle wasn't having any of it. He roared like a fucking tiger and revved up that old pickup and rammed that little car.

Joey's wife was trying to start it up and get out of his way but she had no traction. She started to fishtail and Kyle bulldozed the car right over the drop-off."

Sandy squeezed her eyes shut. When she opened them she saw a woman with grey hair and glasses sitting in the front seat of a shiny Land Rover. The woman was looking at her quizzically. Sandy turned away and kept listening.

"There's no beach there to speak of and that little Toyota hit the shallows and rolled into the deep water. It was high tide, the windows were open, and Joey and Arden didn't have time to make a move. They rolled and sank. We could see that little car under the water—see it tumbling over and over, it kept rolling until it was gone.

"Jag hit the roof. He pulled Kyle out of the truck and punched him hard. I thought there was gonna be a fight, but Kyle just kept his head down and took the abuse. 'Ya fuckin' moron,' yells Jag, 'fuckin' moron.'

"Jag took charge. He propped the gas pedal on the truck and we helped him pop the clutch and run it into the bay. It went in fast and sank deep. Kyle wanted to hide the rifles in the bush, but Jag made us wrap everything in fishnet, disguises and all, and when we got away from shore we sunk them in the middle of the channel."

"You make me sick," Sandy said. "Why would you want to do something like that? You live here. The people you robbed—you know them. You know all of them."

"Yeah, well…" Derek looked down at his feet. "Credit unions and stuff… they're insured. Everybody knows that, right?"

"We're loading. Keep your head down." The cars ahead of Sandy started moving. "And keep quiet." She started onto the ramp to the upper parking deck. Derek started talking anyway.

"What's worse, nobody made any money. It turns out the credit union doesn't keep much cash on hand. Jag took Joey's share. Kyle took extra. He said he needed it because he'd lost the guns. I ended up with three hundred and eighty-six dollars. A week later I was back knocking on doors begging for work."

"That's what you killed Arden for? And ruined Joey's life?" *Mine too*, she thought.

He shrugged. "Nothing worked out like it was supposed to."

"Get used to it. Now just shut up." Derek huddled on the floor and Sandy threw her jacket over him. People on the car deck looked at her as she slammed the car door. She stomped up to the snack bar, paid a machine to hork cappuccino at her, and sat in a corner of an outer deck where no one would find her or look at her or talk to her.

That little shit, she thought. Him and Jag and Jag's fat little boy and their greedy fat fingers. And Joey too greedy and fed up and stuckup to resist them, and beautiful Arden, not run off with some rich and sophisticated tourist—like I always secretly hoped—but drowning alone in her rusty old junker at the bottom of Agamemnon Channel, in a matter of seconds yanked from life and friends and sunlight into cold flesh into bone, drifting out to join the prawns and plankton and starfish down on the sea bottom. Meanwhile the rest of us keep showing up for hump night at the Legion.

I could put them all away now with what I know, she thought. Joey too. For a moment her heart went out to Jag. What was it like to have a child, to have someone you're more desperate to protect even than yourself.

She soon got over it. Someday, if Kyle gets to be too much trouble, Jag will just cut him loose.

And with what Derek just told me, I could put them all away. Except that since I convinced Walter to tow the wreck into the deeps, I'm complicit too—an accessory. So is Walter.

She pushed the Escort hard as she could on the long hills up from the ferry terminal. Without a word she dropped Derek at the bus station and headed through town for False Creek, where Walter had told her he moored the *Medusa Deep*.

"There's a place on Broadway," he'd told her, "where we can go out for a few drinks. There's even a dance floor if you're inclined."

What was she getting herself into? she asked herself. "Some fun," she answered aloud as she stopped at a light on West Second with the engine muttering and the radio on. No more talk about Joey or Arden or any other people dead or brain-damaged or needy or hopeless in any way. That would be the rule this weekend.

"Then," said Walter, "I've got some tickets to an excellent concert—I think you'll enjoy it."

How about some dinner? Sandy thought. White wine and something with lots of fresh greens. It's been a long time. Dammit, I am going for it. Some fun for a change.

62. The man who went into the water

The lady's car twisted back onto the road, gravel scorching the pavement under its wheels, and then the car was gone with her in it. It was like Walter said. The farther you swim, the deeper the water gets. After a point the far shore gets no closer. You start to wonder if you really want to get there. One by one, you can't see the people around you any more. They have got as far as they're going to go. You keep swimming, all the time more and more alone.

And then you feel a current, colder than all the others, tugging at your feet. Because from way down in the dark among the ghosts and glowing shapes and wrecked boats and bones at the bottom of the strait, something big is coming up.

I pushed the red button that opened the main gate. Inside, a woman at the front desk told me the code I would need to remember to get out. It was dead easy.

Inside it was like a hospital where a lot of the patients were up and about, talking with regular people from the outside, even though they were mostly old. The people in pyjamas and dressing gowns were patients and the people dressed in day clothes were not. There were a lot of people sitting around in chairs not talking to anyone or particularly doing anything.

At last I find the right room and who is there but Rose's son Rory.

"Hey," he says. We look at Rose.

"She's been out for a while," Rory says. "It comes and goes."

Rose is asleep, a plastic mask over her mouth and nose. Her eyelids flutter as if she's dreaming or pretending to dream.

"Is this a good time for me to come here?"

Rory yawns deeply and his eyelids flutter like his mum's. He is a big paunchy guy who resembles his dad. "It's a great time," he says. "If you wanna hang in here, I'm going down the road for some coffee and sausage rolls."

"I brought flowers." Without a word he takes the little vase of flowers from me and puts it on the night stand beside the bed, with another bouquet behind a fence of pink and green cards.

"If you want to visit my mom," he says, "now is a good time."

I look around. There are other people in the room. Rose, who is sleeping, faces a bed where a fat lady with gray hair and a plastic mask is sitting up and looking at us. Another lady, younger and with red hair, is sitting beside her bed and also looking at us. Next to them is another bed with a girl sitting on the side, skinny and with a kind of towel wrapped around her head, and next to Rose's bed is a white curtain. Rose is still asleep. As I look around Rory looks around too. He is embarrassed and so am I. Everyone but Rose is looking at us.

"I guess we are handsome guys," I say.

"Dad's coming in a while," Rory says. "The whole family's coming down here in shifts. You need a ride back home?"

"When is Rose going to wake up?"

"She's awake now," he says. Then he leans over and whispers "Mom's stoned to the eyeballs so don't expect a whole lot."

Sure enough Rose is looking at me. Her head bobs up, dazed and wobbly like a baby bird. Rory says back in a bit mom and is gone. "Joey?" Rose says. "What are you doing here? Heading for the ferry?"

"The woman who brought me here," I say. "She had to get to the ferry. It's just that I thought…"

"The ferry…" Rose continues. "It's supposed to move but you know, it doesn't move. It just sits there. Isn't that the funniest thing?"

"I don't think I've ever been on the ferry, that I recall." I reach for her water bottle. "Do you want some water?"

"It remains stationary." Rose takes a sip, her lips fumbling around the straw. She lies back and looks at me.

Rose is always slim, but now she is so skinny it's ridiculous. She stretches her arms out—one of them has a needle stuck into it, plugging her in to a long tube full of clear liquid. It is like a toy version of the hoses we have at the plant, and for all I know, that clear liquid is clean life-giving seawater. I lean over to hug her, lying there in the bed. "My big Joey," she says, as if I am her kid too. "You feel so big and strong."

"I've been getting a good workout on the day crew. It's better in some ways than fingerpacking. But I miss all the people on the night crew."

"There's always next year," Rose says.

"We like you better as the straw boss. Barb is way harder to get along with."

"Barb's in her glory. She's wanted to be plant manager for years. Now she can have the job of her dreams and get all the headaches."

"I hope you come back next year." Rose winces. "Does it hurt?" I say, remembering what the woman said. She was kind of a bitch about it, but maybe she was right.

Rose's arm is like a spider's leg when she reaches out for her plastic bottle. She sips a few drops of water and says, "The morphine messes up my brains. I can't make sense of anything I say. It's like being married to myself—there's two of me and it's the clueless, embarrassing one that does all the talking. The only time I feel clear in my mind is when the pain hits—it stabs and burns—or when I get the urge for a smoke."

"Well Rose if you want a smoke now, I guess I can help you outside."

"Joey hon, I would just love that. But why don't we stay here, and you sit with me, and hold my hand for a minute."

Later I said, "Rose I thought you were asleep!"

Rose and I are still holding hands, but because she fell asleep I was going to leave. Normally people's hands would be sweaty, holding them that long, but Rose's hand is dry. I can feel her heat, but the thing inside her sucks up all her sweat and all mine too.

She's looking at me brightly and says, "For all I know, I am asleep."

"Since I busted the freezer, some of the guys started calling me Commander Zero the super hero."

"You're my big Zero," Rose says. "Do you have any idea how crazy I was about you?" Her eyes are wet. "I never felt anything like it."

Rose reaches out and takes my hand. "I would have gone anywhere," she said, "If you asked me. I was just... crazy like a teenager, and I knew I was being stupid and I couldn't help it."

Rose squeezes my hand, but when I squeeze back she winces. I apologize.

"My big Commander Zero," she says. "And you don't remember a thing about us do you? About us being together."

Out the window I can see mountains. In this place the mountains slope to the sea. The mountains are like the shoulders of women, their long arms reaching under the water. They are searching for something there.

"Maybe that's why this is happening to me," she says, "I'm a bad person and I'm getting what's coming to me."

"I… I don't know why you say that."

"I told her what you were doing, in fact I well, exaggerated. It was too late to stop you from what you were going to do, so I told her that you and the boys had cooked up this crazy *heist* and that you were going to meet Jag in the bay and that if things went bad, Jag was going to smuggle you on his boat, down to the States. So she would think that even if you got away with the robbery, she would lose you. I told her how to get to Revenant Bay, how to find the road, which fork to take."

Now Rose looks at me like a witch cursed by her own magic.

"The road," I say.

"I knew all about it, because you trusted me," she says. "Fetch it out of the drawer there." She has a little nightstand beside her hospital bed. I open the drawer. There is a big brown envelope in there. Just like at the plant Rose always gives clear instructions, spoken or written, and I read these out loud.

"DO NOT OPEN," I read. "PASS ON."

"I wrote it so huge," said Rose. "I'm losing my marbles—if it's not the pain driving me crazy it's the dope making me dopey. PASS ON, what a thing to say, I should've wrote GIVE instead."

"Either way Rose, I'm..." I was totally confused.

She fidgets with her hands, clasping them and unclasping them. "Turn it over."

"TO..."

JOSEPH WINDEBANK the writing says, and there is a phone number and address.

This is some kind of a present for me. "Can I open it now?" I ask.

"Don't get excited luv, it ain't Christmas. Keep an eye out to make sure nobody's watching."

In fact, practically everybody is watching, but they can't see what is between me and Rose. I hunch over to protect the envelope while I rip the end open. Stuff falls out.

"I knew because you came to me and told me. You knew anything could happen and didn't want to carry any ID so you asked me to keep them."

I open the wallet. Everyone calls me Joey or Joe or Zero, but I have never seen my name in print in so many places. Driver's licence, BC medical, and some other plastic cards. What is a Costco? But I am excited: there is even one of those Legion member cards with the stripe that opens the door to get into the bar. I am excited to see that. If I had that, I would not have to get buzzed to get into the Legion, I could get in myself...

There is not too much else. A picture of a smiling woman, and behind her the waiting ocean.

Rose looks away when I pull out the picture. "...wallet, key ring and that's it." She shrugs. "What more do you have in life?

"But I'm a jealous woman and I've got a bad streak, vindictive. I don't know why else I would have told that girl, I liked that girl. Arden."

"You made a mistake maybe," I say. I'm not quite keeping up with her. "At the plant, you always tell me we're allowed to do that."

"I wanted to make some trouble." She smiles at me. "I know what was between us—it was fun for you wasn't it? I've never been so nuts in my life. I used to dream you'd ask me to run away with you. California or Mexico or the east coast, I didn't care." She sinks back into the pillow.

"But it was all just fun for you," she says.

Without asking her I put the wallet and the keys in my pocket. Rose has closed her eyes again. There are tubes in her arm, one of them plugged into a thing that looks like my TV remote. Here I am, I think, saying goodbye to Rose, and in the deepest parts of the saltchuck the leader is bringing together his people. "We have survived everything they have rained down on us and if the world ends," he boasts, "still we will survive."

The heat is fading from her hand. As Rose walks through the forest, voices call to her from underneath the deadfalls and the ferns and the salal. They will stay there forever, haunting the forest at night, scaring the living with their confusion and fear. But Rose is not scared. That light that she can see through the trees, that light is the ocean. Pushing her way through the forest—it's never easy to leave the forest and break out onto the shore. There is always a barrier of rocks and shattered logs and nettles and it is never easy to break through, but Rose breaks through and I can see her, she is perched on the rocks. The air is so dry, the bones of her back tight under her burning skin. First afraid to slide beneath the canopy of her new world. There is always one more thing to do, one more thing that has to be put back in its place, or leave that one thing unfinished forever. She leans forward until nothing can stop her.

Rose reaches for me and takes my hand. "We were the harbour's favourite secret," she says. I look at her hand and I think of the times I have needed Rose and depended on her to stick up for me and even got scared when she was mad, but look at this, look how big my hand is around hers. And her hand is pale—she has been out of the sun, and when I put my hand around her hand, it is like a cloud over the moon.

"And we will survive, even if the world does not end!"

I can hear her voice: we shouldn't be doing this and a man's voice: Can't you ever be bad, just a little bit. Then he kisses her. Her tongue warm and her mouth tasting like cigarettes. I had a picture in my head of some guy doing this, and now I feel like I can recognize this guy.

Rose now has her eyes tight shut. I say, "You know, I wonder… I think I am remembering it now."

"It hurts," she says, and shakes her head. "Damn, they need to up my dose. Push the button." I look around for the button but now Rose has gripped my hands tight. "*Fuck.* Don't let go of me," she says. I free one hand and grope around in the sheets. What button? Rose pulls herself up to cling onto me. I put my arm around her. Then a big woman is beside me again.

"We need to get her back onto the bed," she says. Rose is gripping so hard it starts to hurt. I grip her right back. "Don't let go of me," she says.

"I'm sorry it hurts," I say. She makes a whimpering sound.

Then someone says, "Sir, we've got to get proper access to the patient."

Rose holds her lips tight. There is a sound like an animal in there. It is all she can do to keep that sound from coming out, so she can still be the person we know, named Rose, and I think, if…

The ladies get Rose to lie back on her pillows, but she is still gripping onto my hand.

The voices of the women are louder, they are coming to greet her. From every side the waters are rising and rushing in and the room is losing its shape and the walls are falling away, darker and darker the water until Rose is gone from sight, deeper and deeper her hands her arms her hips her bones—her bones mix with the bones of the great beasts, there is a dark country down there under the water and they are waiting for Rose to join them. Sliding easily through the dark water they are huge creatures—they are full of self-esteem because they do not imagine they are anything except what they are, and what they have always been.

But then another change will come. The body changes, it changes into bone into beast into water and then changes into body again—my dreams are creatures waiting for this change, and so are the great birds that circle over the cliffs, calling to each other in their cold voices, and so are the women who walk the forests in the night, and so are the mountains that are reaching down under the water—there is something they can't see, something that's in the shadows there—and so am I, I think, so am I. I am looking at my hand around her hand.

"Those birds," I say, "those birds are gone from the cliffs."

"Don't let go," says Rose.

"I used to hear them up there. But now, I think they've flown someplace else."

I can feel the women around me, the heat from their bodies as they come closer. "I know you're her friend," the one woman says, "but you should really give us some space here." They are putting out their hands, they are reaching and searching for her and I hear one of them call my name.

"Joey," the nurse says. She scoops something off the floor and offers it to me. "This just fell—it's yours?"

She is holding my wallet. I look at it.

"Because if it's yours," the woman says, "you should take it."

I am still holding Rose's hand in mine.

"Hello?" The woman says. "Anybody home?"

I have to reach forward to take what the woman is handing to me. So then I let go.

Acknowledgements

I was shocked, believe me: in the midst of a bitter, penny-pinching March, I received an Ontario Arts Council Works-In-Progress grant to rebuild my skeletal *Commander Zero* manuscript into a book. Desperately I scanned the paperwork for the names of friends among the jury members (although hey, I'm sure that government granting procedures are bristling with anti-nepotism safeguards) but I didn't see any familiar names; no one who could be accused of having, for any reason, a soft spot for David Lee.

This vote of faith—four complete strangers had judged my writing worthy of support—was as bracing as the money itself, and its memory frequently recharged my morale during the ensuing months, and years, as I whipped "Zero" into shape and tried to get it into print. During that time yet another Works-In-Progress grant, and a Creative Writing grant from the Canada Council, proved essential aids to keeping the wolf from the door while I juggled jobs and other writing projects, and tried to remain for those around me a half-decent husband, father and friend. I am grateful for this support.

In the same period, Beverly Daurio of The Mercury Press allowed me an OAC Writers' Reserve grant which I also acknowledge, but this is only a small part of Bev's generosity towards "Zero" and myself. Years ago, when we were both Toronto small-press publishers, Bev was already urging me to write more, and she was kind enough to read and critique a recent draft of this manuscript. Charlie Huisken also gave me important feedback on a later draft, as did my wife Maureen Cochrane and my sister Jacqueline Lee.

An early version of *Commander Zero* was also critiqued by both Marion Johnson of London, Ontario and Mari-Lou Rowley of Saskatoon—both busy at their own writing, as well as other things, both of whom took the time to read that short version and give detailed answers to my hapless "might I have a book here, or what?" As writer-in-residence at McMaster University in 2003, Marlene Nourbese Phillip was also supportive after reading parts of an early draft. Prior to this Anne-Marie Camilleri and Nadine Pedersen gave instructive feedback when "Zero" was no more than fragments.

But whatever else one can say about *Commander Zero*, although it is fictional throughout, it is a novel based on lived experience. A happily-urbanized small-press publisher / editor / musical couple such as myself and Maureen, raising two young sons, who happen to wind up in a place like Pender Harbour, BC, have no reason to expect any sort of welcoming committee. The Harbour might look like paradise, but it can be an impenetrable paradise and many new arrivals soon depart, or linger for decades never feeling fully accepted. But to integrate into a working community, you have to work in and with it and dare not only to commit and contribute, but to depend on it for all kinds of support including your daily livelihood. There is a long list of people who went out of their way to help us work to survive and to make a rewarding lifestyle for ourselves in Pender Harbour. Specifically for helping me cultivate my working relationship with these passages and inlets and rocky shores, I must single out for thanks Les Fowler, Ted Woodard and Bill Sutherland for many contributions; Diana

Pryde at the Harbour Authority; Hazel Reid and Doug Beguin at Pender Harbour Seafoods; Rick Jerema who hired me for a season out on the water; and, of course, the folks at Towns Netting and Marine Supply in Steveston, BC.

This book is a work of fiction, and any resemblance between its plot or characters, and any real-life incidents or persons living or dead, is purely coincidental. The author has done his best to stay true to the character of Pender Harbour and the Sunshine Coast, but in the interest of the narrative, has taken liberties with certain geographic details. He hopes that local readers will forgive the occasional unfamiliar shoreline, bay or back road. Many of the places mentioned in *Commander Zero* actually exist, but since this is a work of fiction, some do not.

Author Biography

Originally from Mission, BC, after graduating in English from UBC David Lee spent many years in Toronto where he performed, toured and recorded as a double bassist and cellist, worked for the jazz magazine *Coda*, and ran the small press Nightwood Editions. His books include *Stopping Time: Paul Bley and the Transformation of Jazz* (Véhicule Press 1999), *The Battle of the Five Spot: Ornette Coleman and the New York Jazz Field* (The Mercury Press 2006) and the award-winning *Chainsaws: A History* (Harbour Publishing 2006). Currently, while pursuing a PHD in English at the University of Guelph, he lives with his family in Hamilton, Ontario.